Glimmer

Yovette B Brooks

WESTBOW
PRESS

PRESS

A DIVISION OF THOMAS NELSON

WestBow Press books may be ordered through booksellers or by contacting:

WestBow Press
A Division of Thomas Nelson
1663 Liberty Drive
Bloomington, IN 47403
www.westbowpress.com
1-(866) 928-1240

Because of the dynamic nature of the Internet, any Web addresses or links contained in this book may have changed since publication and may no longer be valid. The views expressed in this work are solely those of the author and do not necessarily reflect the views of the publisher, and the publisher hereby disclaims any responsibility for them.

ISBN: 978-1-4497-0427-8 (sc)
ISBN: 978-1-4497-0426-1 (dj)
ISBN: 978-1-4497-0475-9 (e)

Library of Congress Control Number: 2010933985

Printed in the United States of America

WestBow Press rev. date: 9/9/2010

Contents

Glimmer—A faint glimpse of things yet to come.

"But I am the very essence of health," I shouted at the doctor. "I watch what I eat, I exercise, I don't smoke or drink. I have never even taken a drug in my life. How can I have cancer?" I knew he was doing his best, but I just couldn't believe it. I was in total shock.

"Listen to me, Lindsey. I know you're healthy and do your best, but some things just can't be helped. They just seem to come out of nowhere and for no reason. You would be one of my last patients that I would have ever thought would have cancer." Doc Harvey was patting my arm. He was a nice older gentleman with graying hair and a very pleasing smile, when he saw me normally for my yearly check up. But today the smile didn't cut it. He was trying extra hard to be sweet and comforting, but it really wasn't helping.

Chapter 1

Depression and Determination

There were just two things I was sure of: cancer can kill you, and I had it...

It was dark when I opened my eyes. What had happened? Where was I? It took me a few minutes to remember. Oh, why did I have to remember? Why couldn't I get amnesia or something, just forget everything, especially the last week? Why couldn't it just be a horrible nightmare? The lights dancing lightly on my wall told me my door was open and Dad had to be watching TV in the living room. I pulled myself up, but I felt cold and hollow, like an empty shell. I threw my feet off the bed and onto the floor.

"Lindz?" I heard Dad call from the living room. "Come here. We need to talk." I took a deep breath and headed up the hall. "Sit down, babe," he said.

"Dad, I really don't feel like talking about this." I slumped down on the couch and hugged my knees into my chest.

"I know," he said, "but we have to. It is not going to go away on its own. We need to take action now! There are so many new treatments since your mom passed away."

I looked up at Dad. His aura was the palest of blues; it almost had a light green cast to it. How hard this had to be on him. I was sure all this was making him sick, and his color confirmed it. He looked like he hadn't slept since the doc gave us the news. His eyes had large, dark circles under them; he looked like was trying to grow a beard, it had been so long since he had shaved; and his hair was messy, too. I looked around and realized how life had just come to a halt since the doctor's diagnosis. I could see the trash running over in the kitchen, the dishes piled on the cabinet, the filthy floor —and all this because I had fainted one day in gym class. Life sucked! It didn't a week ago—it had been great—but now, it just sucked!

"Lindz?" I turned and looked back at Dad and I could see he was fighting the urge to fall apart. It had been ten years since mom died of cancer. She was sick for a long time. Our lives had changed a lot since then. Dad had quit smoking and started doing the health thing. He got me into every sport he could, and we had gone from your average couch potato family to the pentacle of health.

"Yeah, Dad." He had been doing his best.

"There is a research hospital in Kentucky that Doc Harvey has put me in contact with. A Dr. Jenkins is head of the cancer wing and there has been some great advancement in his department."

I raised my head. "Kentucky ..."

He kept on. "Yes, Kentucky. We have an appointment with the doc on Wednesday, so you need to get packed."

Wednesday. What day was it? I wasn't even sure. "What is today?" I asked.

"Monday. Oh, yeah. Beth has called every day, but I just keep telling her you are sick and in bed. You may want to call her."

I nodded and pulled myself up. What was I going to tell her? Beth had been my best friend since we were eight. I walked slowly back down the hall and into my room. I didn't know how to even start to tell her. She was the one that kept me going after mom died. The sun was coming up. My floor looked orange from the sun spilling in. I looked over my shoulder to the clock on my chest. 5:30 a.m. Well, at least I didn't have to call her right now. As I turned back around, I saw my reflection in the mirror. What color was I? Why didn't I ever see an aura around myself? Was I yellow, like Mom was when she was dying? Why was I the only one that saw auras? I had always seen them, ever since I could remember, but I never saw my own. I looked at my reflection. I was a wreck. My hair was as bad as Dad's. No, maybe worse. Mine was longer. The circles under my eyes looked worse than Dad's. The last few days were really just a blur of anger, sadness, and then hopelessness. I felt so utterly hopeless. What if I just dropped to the floor, curled up in a ball, and let myself die? I really didn't want to fight; I saw what it had done to Mom. She had been pretty healthy. Well, not at the top of her game, but not bad, and then ... all the meds, all the chemo, all the treatments, and for what? It didn't help her in the end. It just made her sick and miserable. I didn't want to die that way. I was healthy, or at least I felt healthy; I didn't show any signs of being sick. I looked at my reflection in the mirror again. Well, I was healthy except for the fainting spell that led them to the cancer. The cancer that was stealing my life, my dreams. Okay, it's back to hopeless again! I lay back on the bed. What was I going to tell Beth? She should be up in an hour, but by six I couldn't wait any longer.

I could do this. No, I am not sure.

"Hello?"

Hang up! Hang up! my head was yelling. Too late.

"Lindsey, are you feeling better? I haven't seen you in days. Your dad said you were in bed sick. What's the matter?" Beth was concerned. You could hear it in her voice.

"Just some kind of bug, I think. I am fine, but I just thought I would call you and tell you we are heading out of town for a couple of days. Doc said I was a little stressed out, so that's why I fainted in gym the other day. So now, Dad has some weird notion of taking off for a while." There was a silence for a moment.

"Lindz, this is me, Beth. What's wrong?" She knew me all too well to fall for that.

"I really don't want to talk about it now, Beth. I will call you when we get back and then maybe, just maybe, I will have a grip on it myself and I will be able to tell you everything, but I am just not ready yet, okay?" I took a deep breath.

"It must be bad. I will give you a week, and if I haven't heard from you, I will track you down. You hear me? And you know I will, so whether you're back or not, I will be expecting your call."

"Thanks, Beth. I knew I could count on you. You're the best." I needed to get off the phone. "I'll talk to you in a week. Okay. Love ya. Bye." I hung up without waiting for her response, but I knew I was about to fall apart on her. I calmed myself then pulled my bag out of the closet and started packing. I really didn't care what went in; it didn't matter—nothing mattered. Why did I have to go? I threw the bag on the floor and curled up on the bed. Tears flowed down and I just let the black take me.

I saw Mom, her face so clear and so beautiful. It was before the cancer, before all the treatments. I watched her sit in her favorite chair in front of the TV. Time stood still for a moment. Then everything moved in slow motion, from the day she came home from getting the news to the pain that she felt taking all the medication and chemo. I also saw Dad as he struggled to stay strong for me. I remembered her telling me things were going to be fine and not to worry. I saw the visitors come and go; Reverend Carr and his wife, our neighbors and friends. I saw all the way to her last day. She was still so beautiful, but worn. She put on her best smile for Dad and me, but you could see the pain in her eyes; they were so weak. She always had told me that God had a plan. Some plan. How anyone could believe in a god that let people die like that ... The funeral and the days that followed passed before me. The depression that Dad went through. It took him months to recover.

I woke in tears and sweat. I did not want Dad to have to suffer like that again. What could I do? I sat up on the bed. I was going to have to get up, stop falling apart, and make the best of it for Dad's sake. He was already in pain, and if I showed it, then it was going to be that much harder on him. I stood up, and for the first time in ten days, I felt a sense of peace come over me. I was going to put my foot down. I was not going to fall apart again. I had to be strong for Dad. Now I understood Mom's smile at the end. I knew it was for us, but until now, I really didn't fully understand why she tried so hard not show the pain she was in.

I picked up my bag off the floor and dumped it on the bed. I was going to look good. I wasn't going to let it show, not in what I wore, how I held my head. No, I was going to be strong. If I didn't have long to live, well, I was going to live! I wasn't going to let them take what time I did have and throw me in a bed and stuff drugs down me so I didn't want to move. I wanted to live for the time I had left. Do things I have never done, go places I had never gone. No, I wasn't going to let them ruin what time I had left, however long that might be. I felt the hopelessness of the last week fall off me. I stood strong and determined. I was not going to give in to hopelessness, not going to give in to the sickness that threatened my life. No! I wasn't going to give Dad more heartache by watching me suffer and die like Mom. I was going to live like I was not sick. I didn't care how much it cost me, I was not going to let Dad see me sick and weak. I turned and headed up the hall.

Dad was sitting in the kitchen, not really doing anything, just sort of sitting there staring off into space. I knew his mind was probably reliving Mom's death. "Dad?" I patted him on the arm then kissed him on the forehead. "I need to say something and I need you to let me say it, no interrupting." I went around the table and sat across from him so I could look him in the eyes. They were puffy and red. I knew he was already in pain. He just looked at me. "I have made a decision. I know you are probably not going to like it, but I have made up my mind. I don't want to end up like Mom. I am healthy and I want to live what time I have left living, not suffering like her. They shoved so much stuff down her, and it was just suffering. And none of it helped." As I spoke, a tear ran down Dad's cheek, but he held his tongue. "I will go to this guy in Kentucky, but that will be the only one. We will just see what he says, but I have made up my mind. I am not going to just let them kill me from a bed, Dad. I want to live for the time I have left. I want to make it the best time ever."

Dad gave me a weak smile. "Let's take it one step at a time. We will see what this Jenkins says and we will go from there, alright?"

I was glad he hadn't fussed or insisted I was wrong, but he had let me speak and said okay in a way, but left it open just in case. For the first time, I realized I was starving. I couldn't remember the last time I had eaten.

"You hungry? I can't remember the last time I ate, how about you?" I asked. I got up and went to the fridge.

"How about we go out?" Dad said as he got up from the table.

I turned and smiled. "Sounds good to me."

Chapter 2

Confusion

The plane ride to Kentucky wasn't that long, but when you're waiting, it always seems like forever. Under other circumstances, I think Dad would be thrilled about going since Mom had attended the University of Kentucky and we were both big Wildcat fans. I brought a bunch of magazines that I bought when went out and ate the night before. They were all on traveling. I started making a list of things I wanted to do and see. It was sort of funny; I wanted to see and do things others would have thought crazy. I wanted to see historic places, hike the Grand Canyon, and visit Mount Rushmore. Go horseback riding on a beach. I scribbled in a journal I had bought. Dad looked over to see what I had written once and smiled. "Don't you want to go to Rome or Paris or somewhere like that?"

"No, not really," I said, and I didn't. I wanted to be normal. These were things I had always wanted to do—and of course, going to Rome or Paris would be great—but I would rather spend my time doing things I had always wanted to do. I loved nature, even though we lived in a city. I spent lots of time in the park and we were always going camping. So that's what I wanted: to camp, to spend time with nature and with Dad. I felt good about my list, felt good about my decision not to die from a bed. By the time we landed, I had written down several state parks and other sites I wanted to visit or see.

Airports are not fun; going through security, finding your luggage, and then getting your car or taxi. It took us over an hour just to get to the front doors of the place. It took us another forty minutes to get our car and get on the road. Luckily, the car had GPS or we would have never found the place. It was huge. It looked more like a university than a research hospital, but I guess it was really both together. We stopped, parked, and then walked all over the place looking for this man's office. Our appointment was at 5 p.m. and we were cutting it close. Just as we were about to give up, we found a security guard and he gave us directions. We were five minutes late, but at least we made it.

"Sorry you got so lost," the receptionist said. "I was starting to get a little worried." She showed us down a hall to two large doors. "Go right in. He is expecting you." When the door opened, there was an unmistakable awe that you felt; the office was huge. It was really two floors. One floor had a lab and all that goes with it: microscopes, Bunsen burners, and then all the really cool stuff that looked like a CSI lab from TV. There was a small room tucked away in the corner on the first floor. It had a couch and a huge desk that could be seen through the doorway. There were people moving all about, so we really didn't know where to go. Finally, a young man in a blue lab coat came up to us.

"You the Blacks?" he said as he stopped in front of us.

"Yes," Dad said.

"The doc will be with you in a minute. You can go in there." He pointed to the corner office.

"Thanks," Dad said. And with that, the guy turned and headed back over to the lab area.

"So which one do you think is the doc?" I asked Dad as we walked toward the office. We were both looking around at all the people running here and there.

"No clue. What about you?"

I really had no clue either. I was just trying to keep from bolting out the door. We sat down and found ourselves facing a large window. It was clouding up and the trees out the window were blowing in the wind, but it wasn't storming ... yet.

"Sorry to keep you waiting." A tall slender man came around the couch and stood in front of us. "I was refreshing myself on all the tests and X-rays Dr. Harvey sent me." He stuck his hand out to Dad. "Terry Jenkins."

Dad stood and took his hand. "Matthew Black, and this is Lindsey." He sort of motioned toward me, as if I would be anyone else, since I was the only other one here, and it was about me.

"Nice to meet you both. I wish it could have been under different circumstances." That was refreshing to hear. Dr. Jenkins wasn't very old, I didn't think. Maybe in his early 30s, which sort of seemed out of place. He was nice looking for a lab geek, with sandy blonde hair that had that messy look going, but he pulled it off. "Now, I know you have been through all kinds of tests, and I am afraid to say I would like to do a few of my own. I know that sounds bad, but at most hospitals they just don't do specific-to-the-cause tests, as I like to call them." He talked as if it were nothing, but had a look of concern on his face. The kind that tells you not to feel so bad about his telling you what he was going to do to you. "I just need to take a few tissue samples that I can run tests on to see if I can get a grip on exactly what you have. Now this may sound bad, but some things are treatable and some are not." Well, I was a little taken aback. Most doctors wanted to treat you with something no matter what, but he acknowledged that sometimes you just couldn't do anything. "That doesn't mean we are giving up, it just means that sometimes it's better to be healthy a few more years than live in a hospital trying to cure something we have no idea how to cure." I was so impressed and relieved at the same time that I must have let out a big sigh. "Well, I can see you must feel the same. I was starting to think you didn't breathe for a minute." He looked down at me and smiled.

"That sounded so much better that what I was expecting you to say. I definitely feel the same way." I spoke for the first time.

"Alright then, let's get some tests scheduled for first thing in the morning so we can see what we're up against."

"Will the test be painful" Dad asked Dr. Jenkins as he looked at me. The stress of the whole ordeal was showing on his face. I was sure he was thinking, "here we go again". Mom had been through so many of these kinds of tests.

"She will be under heavy anesthesia and I promise you, she won't feel a thing" he answered in a very reassuring tone as he typed on his computer. "Dr. Harvey told me you lost your wife several years back to cancer".

"Yes." Dad answered, His voice almost cracked.

"We have made great advancements in medicine since then Mr. Black, and I assure you we will do whatever it takes to see that your daughter is healed from this horrible disease". Dad smiled at me. It was nice to see him smile again. Dad and Dr. Jenkins talked as I sat there thinking about how much I dislike tests. I wondered about the tissue samples he mentioned. Were they going to big or small? Was I going to wake up with big patches gone?

That night, I really didn't sleep much, and when I did fall asleep, I kept seeing Mom's face. Finally, I just got up and went out on the hotel balcony and sat. The sun eventually started coming up and it would soon be time to head out. The sunrise was beautiful, one of the best I had seen in a long time. The area was really pretty.

"You ready to go?" Dad stepped out of the door. "We are supposed to be there in thirty minutes."

"I will be ready in fifteen."

Dad looked worn out too. He walked over and put his hand on my shoulder. "Love you, Lindz."

"Love you, too, Dad. I have a good feeling about this doc. He seemed really down to earth." I patted Dad on the hand and smiled up at him. He smiled, but I could see the pain in his eyes. I got up, gave him a quick kiss on the cheek, and headed back in to get dressed. It didn't take me long. I had everything set out in outfits, down to earrings and necklaces. "I'm ready, Dad. Let's go get it over with." I handed Dad his keys, grabbed my purse, and headed for the door.

The place was already busy, even at this early hour. We were met at the front door by Dr. Jenkins himself. "Here we go," he said as he handed Dad a key. "Go up to the second floor to room 243. It's yours for the day. Take advantage of everything in there. You'll need to pass time." He smiled. "I promise I will take good care of her, Mr. Black." And with that, he turned to me. "If you will, Miss Lindsey, follow me."

I gave Dad a quick hug and then followed Dr. Jenkins down the hall. "Can I ask what is in room 243 that's supposed to keep him occupied?"

He gave a quick glance over his shoulder and smiled. "Everything you can think of. It is a set of rooms, really. It has a gym, a sauna, a pool, Internet, satellite TV, about every movie and every kind of music out there. It is a distraction haven." He smiled. "This is going to be harder on him than you. The time will drag by for him. You, however, will be under anesthesia, so the day will be over quickly for you." I smiled back. We went down two more halls and through a big set of double doors where a lady was waiting. "Lindsey, this is Mary. She will be with you all day. She is to keep everything moving smoothly and see to your every need. You may be out, but your body still functions and has needs, and Mary will be the one taking care of you. She is really good at her job, so don't worry about a thing." Mary was pretty, with her dark skin and dark eyes and hair. He looked over at her. "She is all yours until she goes under." He looked back at me. "Any questions?"

I shook my head. "Let's just get it over with."

"Your wish is my command. Mary, she's all yours." With that, he left the room. I turned to look at Mary. She was holding out a bag.

"Take what's in here and put it on. Everything you have on goes in here in its place, and I do mean everything. Don't even leave your earrings on. You can use that room to change." She pointed at a door on the left. "We will put your bag in one of those lockers and I will take the key to your dad until we're done, okay?"

I just nodded and took the bag from her hand. The room was just a changing room; it was tiny. Oh, yuck—a hospital gown. No, it was a little different, with the ties on both the sides. Easy access, I guess. I shuttered just thinking of strangers looking at me. I took a deep breath and opened the door again. Mary just stood there smiling at me. "Don't worry. This day will be over soon."

She took my bag and put it in a locker, then took me to another room with three other people and a table in it. "Lie down and just close your eyes. Jay here is going to put a mask on you, and you just need to relax and breathe." She turned to one of the other guys. "Take this to Mr. Black in suite 243." She handed him the key. He turned and left at once. I lay down and took a deep breath. Jay smiled and put the mask over my mouth and nose.

"Just breathe normally. It usually doesn't take long."

I was a little chilly laying there in a little bitty gown and I shivered. Mary immediately went and opened a cabinet and pulled a blanket out for me. It was heated and felt so warm. She smiled and patted my arm. "It's going to be fine, I promise."

"Lindsey." I heard my name, but wasn't sure where it was coming from. I slowly opened my eyes and blinked a few times, trying to focus them. "Lindsey." It was Dr. Jenkins, and I could see Mary standing there behind him. "Well, that didn't take too long did it?" he asked. I felt like a ton of bricks was on me and really couldn't move. "I know you'll be groggy for a little while, so you just relax and when you feel like you can move or talk, Mary will be here to get you dressed and ready." He patted my arm. I could see him do it, but really couldn't feel it. "You did great today. Now just rest and I will see you again in a little while." He smiled and turned to Mary. "Call me when she's up and moving well."

"Of course, Dr. Jenkins," she said as he turned and left the room. "Well, I talked to your dad just a few minutes ago and told him you were out of testing and it would be an hour or so before you would be fully awake and moving again. I sent Matt up and got your key and a movie. I hope you like *Pride and Prejudice*. It is one of my favorites. You've got to love that Mr. Darcy." She grinned and turned on the TV. She sat down in the recliner next to my bed. I did like this movie. It was one of my favorites, too. I started feeling tingly all over while Mr. Darcy was confessing his undying love for Miss Elizabeth. And by the time she was visiting her friend Charlotte, I was able to move just a little, but not enough that I would trust getting up.

"You really do love him," Mr. Bennet was saying when I was finally able to sit up in the bed. Mary jumped up and was at my side as soon as I started moving.

"I really love that movie, too," I told her. "It is such a great story."

"Well let's see about getting you dressed and up to see your dad." She retrieved my clothes from the locker and helped me get them on. She held on to me just in case I wasn't quite stable yet, and it was a good thing; I almost fell over twice. "Let's walk a bit. That always helps the drugs wear off."

We headed out the door and up the hallway. We went up three floors and walked the halls there, then up another floor and walked the halls there, too. I had to admit that it was helping; the more I walked, the better I felt. "You ready to head to your dad's room?"

"Yeah, I want to see this room he's in. It sounds like paradise. I may never get him to leave." We both laughed.

"It is a great place. I wish my apartment had even just half the stuff that it does." She led us back to the elevator and we went down to the second floor. When the doors opened, it looked just like a floor at a very expensive hotel. The floor was carpeted, there were room numbers, and it was all decorated and pretty. You would never think you were in a hospital. "Here we go. Room 243."

She knocked on the door and it wasn't long before Dad opened it. "Lindz!" He had me in a bear hug before I even had time to speak.

"Hey, Dad."

"I am going to call Dr. Jenkins now. Don't be alarmed if you get queasy from the anesthesia." Mary told me "If you do get sick more than once, pick up the phone and tell the nurse, okay?" She smiled. "I mean it, don't you hesitate to pick up the phone and ask for help." Dad assured her we would and she took her leave.

The room was huge. It looked like a suite at the Plaza or something. "Have you ever seen anything like it?" Dad asked.

"No. Dr. Jenkins said it had everything you could think of in here," I told him.

"He was right. Come on. I will show you around." He took my arm and started ushering me from room to room. "The Cats won against Virginia tonight, so they are in the Final Four!" Dad told me as we walked.

"That's great Dad! I was hoping they would move on." I was sure that watching the game made the time move a little faster for him. The phone rang as we entered the room with all the movies and music. Dad answered. "Alright, we will be expecting him." He turned to me. "The doc is on his way up.

We better head back to the main room." We had just only gotten back to the room when there was a knock on the door. Dad let Dr. Jenkins in.

"I hope you made full use of the room today, Mr. Black."

Dad smiled. "I must admit I did use a lot of it. I need one of those projectors for my house. It was like being right on the sidelines of the game."

Dr. Jenkins smiled. "Good. Yes, those things are great," he said. "Well, all the tests went well and we will be working around the clock for the next twenty-four hours to see what we are up against." He pulled a bottle out of his pocket and handed it to me. "These are pain pills. You won't need one tonight, but tomorrow morning you'll be sore from all the tissue samples we took. So take one in the morning and then another four hours later, then another six hours later, then again eight hours after that. There are only four in there, and that should be all you need." He turned and started talking to Dad.

I didn't notice any bandages on me anywhere, so I was wondering about the samples he had mentioned. I let myself feel my body with all my senses, but it was numb.

"Alright then," Dad was saying. "I guess we will see you tomorrow night." Dr. Jenkins said goodbye and left. "Well, Lindz, let's get back to our room at the hotel. It is getting late."

I hadn't even looked at a clock. What time was it? 9:00 p.m. Could that be right? I glanced out the window and sure enough, it was dark. Well, he was right. It didn't seem like it took five minutes for the day to go by. And despite being out all day, I felt tired. I was looking forward to a hot shower and sleep for the first time in a long while.

The sun was up and bright when I woke. Dad was up and dressed, sitting at the little table in the corner of the room. "You hungry?" he asked.

I went to move, and my body screamed out in protest. I don't think there was a spot on me that didn't hurt. "Pills. I need those pain pills, Dad." He got them off the chest and got a bottle of water out of the little fridge and brought them to me.

"Do you hurt bad?" he asked.

I lied. "Not too bad, but I do hurt enough that I feel like I better take one of those." He opened the bottle and got one out and handed it to me. I thought I might not be able to make myself move, but I did. The pills didn't take long, and I was up and dressed in an hour.

"We are supposed to meet Dr. Jenkins tonight at 7 p.m. at his office, so we have the whole day. Anything you can think of that you might want to do, sweetie?"

A whole day of waiting, I thought. We need to go back to the suite at the hospital. "No, Dad, I don't know what's even around here."

"There are some advertisements on the table over there. I guess we could take a look at those or just drive around 'til we find something."

I smiled. "Let's drive." I grabbed my purse and bottle of pills, and he grabbed his keys and we headed out the door.

"Mr. Black? Lindsey?" I heard a voice coming across the parking lot. "I am glad I caught you." It was Mary. "Dr. Jenkins forgot to give these to you yesterday, so I brought them right over." She handed an envelope to Dad. "Well, you guys have a good day now." She turned and headed back to her car.

Dad opened the envelope. "You have got to be kidding me."

"What is it, Dad?"

He smiled and held up two tickets. "Game tickets to the Final Four ballgame today. We are going to see the Kentucky Wildcats play ball!" Dad was so in seventh heaven. I must admit I wouldn't mind seeing them play either. "The game is at 1 p.m. and it's 9 a.m., so we have a few hours. Let's see what this city holds." He ushered me to the car with a smile. It was good to see him smile a true smile. He had been putting up smiles, but they were just skin deep. This smile showed in his eyes, and it was good to see it.

The day moved by. We ate breakfast and went on our drive. We found an art museum and took enough time there to get a bite to eat and head to the game. The game was great. It had two overtimes and was close. We won by two points. The best game ever, Dad had said over and over again. We found a local park and walked for awhile, then we went and ate. It was just thirty minutes until time to see the doc.

Mary met us at the door. "You're a little early, but that's okay. Come on in and I'll tell Dr. Jenkins you're here." We walked over and sat down on the couch in the small office again. I looked around and noticed a picture over on a shelf. It wasn't big, but it was in a beautiful frame. It was a wedding picture, but I couldn't make out the people until I got up and walked over to it. It was Dr. Jenkins and Mary. So Mary was his wife. She was in a great dress, one of the prettiest I had ever seen. There were people behind them and he had her in a dip. I guessed it was at their reception. They looked so good together, a match made in heaven.

"So, how was the game?" Doc Jenkins asked as he came in. "I was a little preoccupied and didn't get to watch."

"Oh, you missed a heck of a game. We won by two and it was double overtime. Thanks for the tickets," Dad said and stood up to greet him.

"Mary and I hardly ever miss a game, but we had more pressing issues today and I didn't want our tickets to go to waste. I am glad you enjoyed them." He had given us his own tickets; no wonder they were right on the floor.

"It was a really great game. Sorry you didn't get to go," I told him. "Oh, don't you worry about that. It was just a game. This is life or death, and it trumps a game every time." He walked over and sat down behind his desk. Dad sat back down, too. "Well, let's see. Where do we start?" He shuffled through some papers. "Here we go." He looked up at me. "I have not seen a strain quite like this, although all cancers are different, this one seems a little more different than any I've seen before. It is all throughout your lymph nodes, so that means it's everywhere, but yet it doesn't seem to be attacking your organs."

"This is good. Right?" Dad asked Dr. Jenkins

"Yes." He looked at Dad.

"So what exactly does this mean?" I asked.

"Well, to be honest, I am not so sure myself. Let me clarify a little. Since it is in your nodes, we can't do anything to it, but since it's not attacking your organs, we really don't need to. And we really don't need to worry about anything until it does. And then at that point, we will have to just see what it does. I am really sort of baffled as to why it's not attacking. It is ... well ... it's like it's hibernating or something. It's present everywhere in your body, but it's just there. If that makes any sense." He had a puzzled look on his face.

"So what is she supposed to do?" Dad asked.

"Well, I took enough samples to work with for a while, but I say go home and carry on life as normal because until it attacks, there is really nothing wrong. I would suggest you keep in top health, though. Maybe cool it a little while until your body completely heals from all the testing, maybe a week or two, then you can go back to normal. As to why you fainted, I am not really sure, but if it happens again, call me immediately."

My head was spinning. Was I dying or was I not? "So am I dying or not?" I blurted out.

"To tell you the truth, I am not sure. As long as the cells stay in hibernation, you will be fine. But if they ever come out, well at that point ... well, let's just say that I don't think you'll be around a month later. That's just because of the fact that they are everywhere. We did not find one place that the cells weren't present."

I was speechless. So what do I do, go home, act like this never took place? Dad and Dr. Jenkins' conversation was just a mumbled blur for awhile. I just sat thinking. I thought I was dying, but was I? Would I wake up one day and feel sick and die in a month? Would I live long or not? I was confused now. I was planning on going and doing all those things I never got to do yet, but now I wasn't sure what to do. "Do you have any idea what kind of timetable we are looking at?" I interrupted.

The doc looked at me. "No, I really don't."

Mary had come in and sat down beside me and I hadn't even realized it. Not until now did I even realize there was someone holding my hand. I turned and looked her in the eyes. "What should I do?"

She gave me a hug. "Live, sweetie. Don't worry about this. As far as we know, you have your whole life ahead of you. Now go home and live like it. Don't worry about what might happen, because there is nothing you can do until it does. Don't waste your life waiting or thinking about it. Just live." She looked over at her husband.

"She is right. You need to not worry about this, not yet. Let's say in six months you come back and we will see how the cells look and go from there. But if you start getting sick, come back and we will see what's happening. Until then, well, she's right. Just live."

Dad and Dr. Jenkins talked some more. I sat with Mary on the couch and just wondered. What's next? Isn't this what I wanted? They weren't going to try to throw me in a bed or anything. Live! They had said "just live." Just what I wanted to do. So why was I still in disbelief about the whole thing? Maybe Dr. Harvey had been wrong about the cancer. No, he couldn't be. Dr. Jenkins said I had some form of it, he just wasn't sure what.

"It's a lot to take in, I know," Mary said beside me. "The best thing you can do is forget about it unless you get sick. What I am trying to say is don't make yourself sick by worrying about it."

I smiled at her. "I don't plan on it. Life is too short for worry." She smiled back at me.

Dad got up. "You ready, Lindz?"

Dr. Jenkins came over and stuck out his hand and pulled me up when I took it. "Things are going to be fine. Stay healthy and strong." He handed me a card. "This has my cell phone, home phone, and the number here on it. Call me if you have any questions, even if you think they are silly ones." He gave me a big smile. Mary gave me a hug and then we left.

Dad and I were both in shock, I think, because neither one of us spoke all the way back to the hotel. When we made it back, Dad got on the phone immediately with the airline. Our tickets had been open-ended since we didn't know how long we were going to be here. Luckily, we were able to get a couple of seats on the flight the next morning.

The trip home was peaceful, something I had missed the last week. Dad slept most of way and I wondered if I was going to be able to wake him up to get off. He hadn't slept much the last two weeks either, but I guess he had gotten a little peace, too, and was now sleeping like a baby. When we got to the airport, I told Dad I would drive us home, but he had insisted he could.

It was about one in the afternoon by the time we got home. I put my clothes away and put my running shoes on. I needed to get out and think, alone. "I am going for a jog, Dad. My muscles are sore and need a stretch."

He looked at me. I could see he wanted to say no, but he didn't. "You got our phone?"

"Yes, I have it. I just need a little 'me' time, Dad. Why don't you go catch a nap?"

He smiled. "Just be careful."

"I will. See you in a bit."

I ran to the park. It was so wonderful to feel alive again. I guess even after saying it wasn't going to get me down, it had anyway, but I did feel a little relief. A little anyway; I still had to wonder if I would wake up one day and then the next I wouldn't. I sat down on a bench as I entered the park. It had been almost two full weeks since I had ran last and I was a little winded, not to mention sore from all the testing, but it still felt good to be out. The sun was warm on my face as I sat there. I watched a couple of robins fight over a worm. As I sat there thinking over the last few days, I realized I would be heading back to school tomorrow, so I had better get the house cleaned back up. I knew once I got back to school I would not have time for much cleaning until I got caught back up on all the work I had missed. So I headed for home.

Dad was already cleaning when I got there. We spent most of the afternoon vacuuming, moping, and cleaning dishes and such. Then we ordered a pizza and sat down and watched a movie together. It turned out to be a great evening. I called Beth right before bed. "No, really, Beth. I am fine. Just stress, nothing to worry about." Why worry her for nothing ... well, maybe nothing.

Chapter 3
The New Guy

School was normal. I had to really work on the Beth thing though; I am not sure she really believed my story about the doc putting me on rest because I was stressed out. Dad had sort of confirmed it, so she was going with it for now, but I got the feeling she was sure that I still wasn't telling her everything.

I had advanced gym last period every day, but I had a note from the doc to be out for a week, then to be on light activity for the next week, and then I could go back to full activity. So this week I was assigned to help Ms. Julie, one of our Guidance Counselors. She mostly had me running errands for teachers, but today she had me working on some computer programs for Ms. Prate, our other Guidance Counselor, since she had been out sick. When I left, Ms. Prate's aura had been quite orange, which was not good sign.

It had just hit me that I hadn't even noticed Dr. Jenkins' or Mary's color. It was kind of strange; I couldn't ever remember not seeing someone's color before. I guess it had to be the stress. I remembered Mom going from her normal bright pink color to the orange sick color to the bright yellow just before she died. I often wondered why I always saw people with color around them. Beth was really the only one who knew about it. She discovered it when Mom was dying. I had kept talking about Mom being yellow and that Grandma had been that way before she died. That was the year Beth and I had become so close. Until she told me, I had thought everyone saw colors like I did. It was really hard not to just tell her everything, but I didn't want her to worry about me.

"Come this way, Matthias. We can go into my office and talk about your schedule then I will have someone show you around the school." I heard Ms. Julie talking to someone as they walked through the office behind me. New student. We only had eight weeks of school left. Wow, changing schools this close to the end of year had to really suck. I turned my chair so I could check out the new guy. I froze. I had never seen silver before. No blue, no green, no brown, but silver, like sparkling diamonds. It took me a minute to get my eyes refocused to see him and not the shiny silver aura around him. He had copper skin and coal-black long hair that hung just below his shoulders. He looked broad-shouldered, maybe six feet tall. His back was to me, so I couldn't see his face. I must have really been staring, because Ms. Julie's eyes and her bright pink aura were suddenly in my face and I turned around quickly. Why was this guy silver instead of blue? What was different about him?

"Lindsey, would you come in here a minute?" It was Ms. Julie calling me into her office. I took a deep breath, got up, and went into her office. When the guy stood up and turned to meet me, I looked into the darkest eyes I had ever seen. They were completely black, like onyx stones. "Lindsey, this is Matthias Johns. Could you show him around the school, help him find his locker, and show him where his classes are located?"

"Oh, yeah. Sure thing, Ms. Julie. No problem." I tried to sound normal, but I turned and walked out of the office without thinking. I then realized what I had done, so I stuck my head back in. "You coming?" He smiled and headed my way. "Well, let's see your schedule."

He handed it to me, but I was still stuck in those eyes. "Is there something wrong? You keep staring. Do I have a booger hanging out of my nose or something?"

I smiled and we both laughed. "I'm sorry. I just have never seen such great eyes. They are beautiful." That part was true. I had never seen eyes like his, but it was the silver that had me really perplexed.

"Uh, thanks."

I finally tore my eyes from him and looked at the paper in my hand. "Looks like we have several classes together. All but Trig and woodshop."

"Well, at least I will know someone in most of my classes then." He gave me a big grin.

"Locker's down this way, 937." I had to really try hard not to stare. I dropped my gaze and we headed down the main hall and turned toward the math wing. "Here it is." I handed back his paper and pointed out the combination to the lock. "You better try it out. I went through three wrong combinations before they finally got me the right one."

He took the lock in his large hands and spun the dial. It opened on the first try. "Well, I guess I got lucky." He opened the locker, looked in, and then shut it back and locked it again. He leaned up against the locker and looked at me. "So, are the people nice here or is it just another battle between all the cliques?"

The question took me by surprise. "Well, I guess we're not much different from anywhere else. You have the normal popular kids, the jocks, the nerds, and all the emo and goth kids. But we all get along okay, I guess. I think everyone just accepts everyone for who they are," I rambled out, but he smiled.

"Well, that that doesn't sound bad."

"So which group do you fall into?" I asked him.

"I try hard not to fall into any of them. I would rather be alone than take sides." Well that was nice to hear, but I wondered if he was just saying that. "What about you?"

"Well, let's see. I don't really fit in any. I have friends from all the groups. My best friend, Beth, hangs with the popular kids, but I really don't hang out with them. They all are too superficial. I like to keep it real. Come on, I will show you where your classes are." I turned and headed back up the hall with him right beside me. I could feel all the eyes on us as we passed some opened doors. I already knew he was going to be quite popular with the girls, not so much with their boyfriends. I chuckled.

"Okay, what's so funny?"

I stopped in front of room 134. "This is your first-period class tomorrow. Trig with Mr. James. He's a great teacher and you will probably like him." I turned and headed on down the hall. He caught up quick.

"You never answered my question."

"I just have a feeling the girls are going to love you and their boyfriends are going to hate you." I giggled again as I said it.

"Oh," was all he said.

Mrs. Kelly was coming up the main hall as we were going to his third period class. Her color was not very bright today. "Love your sweater, Mrs. Kelly," I told her as we passed.

Her color perked up immediately. "Thanks," she said. It still amazed me how one well-placed compliment could lift someone's day. I showed him all the rest of his classes and we headed back toward the office. The dismissal bell rang before we made it back. "I guess I will see you tomorrow, second period." I waved bye and headed toward my locker.

"See you," I heard him say as I headed the other direction.

"Who was that?" I hadn't made it twenty steps when Beth caught up to me.

"New guy."

"Wow, is he gorgeous or what? Is he single? Where did he move from?"

I turned to look at her. She always seemed to be just the prettiest shade of bright pink. "I have no idea. I was just showing him where his classes were." We went on down to my locker and got my things, then we went to Beth's.

"Man, I missed you in gym today. We played extreme Frisbee and we got slaughtered without you."

Dad had been hesitant about letting me drive, so I was riding with Beth. "I need to tell you something when we get to the car." We hurried through the halls and out to the parking lot. As soon as the door shut, Beth turned my way.

"Well, what is it?"

"The new guy, he is silver."

She looked at me. "Silver?"

I had never seen anyone silver before. "Yes, he sort of sparkles. It's really strange."

She fastened her seatbelt and started the car. "Sparkly silver. What do you think it means?"

"I have no clue," I told her as I fastened my seatbelt.

"So when do you go back to work?" Beth asked. I had a job at the local fitness center but was off until the doc said I could go back to full activity.

"Not until next week."

"So what are you doing Friday, then?" Beth asked.

"Not real sure. Dad said something about going hiking, but I don't know. I was thinking of just catching the new Brad Pitt movie."

"Call me and let me know if you do. I have been dying to see that one, too," she said as she turned onto our street. "You really don't know what the silver means?" she asked.

"No, it's just weird. I have been all over several states and have never seen silver before." She stopped the car in front of the house. "I'll see you tomorrow." I grabbed my books out of the backseat, gave her a quick wave, and headed in the house. I had loads of homework. The cancer didn't seem to be killing me, but after missing two weeks of school, the homework might. It was going to be a late night.

The alarm was screaming way too early. I found myself still dressed and on top of my bed with books scattered everywhere around me. Crap. I had fallen asleep doing homework. I was going to be late for school since I had to shower. I usually did that before I went to bed so I wouldn't have to get up so early in the morning. Shower, gather up books, hurry up. I kept going over everything I needed to do in my head as I did each task. I could hear Beth honking out front before I got my books in my bag. "Have a great day, Dad," I hollered as I ran out the front door. "Sorry, Beth. I hope I haven't made us late. I fell asleep doing homework last night." I threw my books in the back and she sped off before I got my door fully closed.

"I thought you were supposed to be under less stress these days? Sounds like it is still running high."

I laughed. "Maybe I need a doctor's excuse from homework."

We laughed as she pulled into the parking lot. We grabbed our books and ran to class. We both had just gotten through the door when the bell rang. "Close," I whispered as we headed to our seats. Another day, I thought. I still felt fine, well, except being a little tired from staying up so late. At least my first class was a breeze. I didn't have to think much in there. When I got to second period, Matthias was talking to Mrs. Hawthorne. His silver glow seemed to really set off her pink. I found my seat and got my notebook and pencil out. This class hinged on how well you took notes, so I always took lots. The bell rang and Matthias headed to the back of the class, where there were only three empty seats. One was behind me and the other two were on the other side of the class. He looked at both then headed my way. He sat down behind me.

"Do you care if I sit here?" he whispered. I gave a quick headshake.

"Today we are going to have an open discussion test over the papers you turned in Monday. Lindsey, your and Matthias's paper are due next Monday. You'll need to go over chapter twenty-four with him. Since he hasn't been here for any of our discussions and since it's so close to graduation, I am going to let you two do a paper together. It needs to be at least twenty pages. It has to have arguments for both intelligent design and evolution, and then your personal opinion at the end. You are both excused to study hall until Monday." I gathered up my books and headed for the door. I could feel Matthias right behind me. "Give this to Ms.

Jones." Mrs. Hawthorne handed me a paper as I went by her desk. Great. Another paper to do. This made four due on Monday. I was right; missing two weeks of school was going to kill me instead of cancer. Matthias was now walking beside me.

"So which are you for?" he asked.

"What?" I had been in my own thoughts so I hadn't really heard what he said.

"Intelligent design or evolution, which do you believe?"

"I'm not sure. Mom was always a churchgoer, but when she died, well, we never went back after that." Matthias followed as I lead us to the library. The study hall room was in the back. I handed Ms. Jones, the librarian, our note and headed for the room. I found a desk and sat down. Matthias sat down beside me.

"What happened to your mom, or can I ask about it?" He had a look of concern on his face.

"It's okay. It was ten years ago when she died. She had cancer really bad."

"I'm sorry," he said as he laid his hand on mine and gave it a squeeze.

I looked up, and he had the most comforting, heartwarming, sorry-for-your-loss look on his face. He removed his hand quickly when I looked down at it. I let my mind wander. I felt so stressed with all these papers, graduation, doctors' visits ... What did the future hold, or did I even have one?

"Lindsey, where are you? You seem to be far away." I could hear him talking, but it almost didn't seem real. I blinked. I was staring directly into Matthias' eyes and they were so peaceful. His voice was so soft and gentle. I wasn't sure if he was actually talking or the voice was coming from inside my head.

"Things have just been crazy lately." I am not sure if I even spoke it out loud.

"Tell me." My mind pinballed from all the doctors to school and then to the future. Then I thought of the guy in front of me. I wanted to know why he glowed silver and sparkly instead of blue like all the other guys. "So, are we meeting this weekend then?"

"What?" I blinked. Matthias was looking at me.

"You okay? You seem a little zoned out." The bell rang.

"I'm fine. Just lost my train of thought." I grabbed my books and headed out the library door. Where had the time gone?

"This weekend?"

"Yeah, that's fine. How about right after school tomorrow? You doing anything then?"

He smiled. "Not a thing."

"Alright then. Beth drops me off at the house right after school." As we talked, we headed to the lunchroom.

"Do you think she would care if I caught a ride to your house?"

I sat my books down on a table. "No, I am sure it will be fine, but I'll ask." He stood there a second, then turned around and looked around the lunchroom. "You're welcome to sit here if you want."

He turned back around and smiled. "Thanks." I headed for the lunch line as he sat down. I got my plate and sat down. Todd and Kayla dropped their books on the table and headed for the line as well. "I thought you didn't hang with the popular kids," he leaned over and whispered as they dropped back into the chairs across the table from me.

"I don't. You saw who was here first." We both laughed. "Matthias, this is Todd and Kayla."

Todd lifted his head. "Hey, man." Kayla just nodded her head. Todd was always a vibrant blue and Kayla a pale pink unless they were standing together. Sarah and Ashley joined the table too, both their normal colors.

"Sarah, Ashley, this is Matthias."

Sarah, not being the shy type, started taking to Matthias. "So, you're the new guy all the little freshmen are so taken with. Well, at least they have good taste." She gave him her ask-me-out smile. Great, I thought. She is going to jump him right here at the table. "So where did you move from?" She sat down on the other side of him and moved her chair really close to his. He glanced over his shoulder at me. I grinned at him and went back to eating.

"France," he answered.

"Wow! What were you doing in France?"

"My bother restores houses, and his last job was in France." Sarah kept scooting her chair a little closer to him and he kept moving his chair back, so he was getting closer to me.

Michelle came running up to the table. "You'll never guess what I heard!" Gossip. That's all it took to get Sarah's train of thought elsewhere.

Matthias leaned over toward me. "I think I am going to go."

"Wait, I'll go with you." I had finished all but my apple. "Just let me take my tray and dump it." He grabbed both our books.

"I'll meet you at the door." As soon as he stood, Sarah's focus changed back to him.

"You leaving already?"

I stood up. "Mrs. Hawthorne stuck us on a project together and it's due Monday. We need to get some research done." She looked at me with her he's-mine look.

"Yeah," he said. "It was nice to meet you guys." Neither one of us waited for any response. I headed for the trashcan and he headed for the door. He handed me my books when I got to the door.

"We've got fifteen minutes before the next class. Come on, I'll show you where to go to get away from their madness." He smiled and fell into step behind me as I headed for the stairs, up to the third floor and to the old wing of the school. "They really don't use this part much anymore, well, except for storage, but there is a spot up here that is great." Why I was showing him my secret spot I really had no idea. Beth didn't even know this spot. Through the old chemistry lab and out a window to a ledge, it looked over part of the city.

"Great view," he said as he slid out on the ledge beside me.

"Yeah, it's great to have some silence sometimes." He stared out over the city. "Now, you can't tell anyone about this spot. No one knows about it. Not even Beth."

He looked at me. "So why did you show me?" he asked.

"No idea, but now that you know about it, mum's the word, okay?"

He leaned over and bumped me with his shoulder. "I am good with secrets." The second lunch bell rang.

"Come on, or we are going to be late." I jumped up and headed through the storage room. He followed. "Here. I noticed you didn't eat anything." I handed him my apple.

He smiled. "Thanks."

We had three more classes together before last period, in which I had gym and he had woodshop. I couldn't understand why I had showed him my spot. I guess it was just an impulse, but maybe it was that I knew he was going to have to get away from Sarah. Of course. That had to be it. It couldn't be anything else. I was in the guidance office again instead of gym, so I was sitting back in front of the computer, but I really wasn't paying attention to it.

Tonight was Thursday night. Dad always went in and got off early on Thursdays, but not tonight. He was pulling some overtime. We were going to have some big medical bills to pay. We hadn't talked or even seen each other much since we had gotten home from Kentucky. He had to take leave without pay when we went, so money was tight and when all the bills came in ... well, we weren't behind yet, but we soon would be, especially with me not being able to go back to work for another week.

"Are you coming?" I looked up to find Beth staring at me.

"What?"

"The bell rang five minutes ago. Where are you these days, Lindz?" She flopped down in the chair next to me.

"I guess graduation and all the work I have to do, and being off work." I think I am more stressed than not stressed."

She looked at me. "What's really bothering you? You have not been the same since you fainted that day in gym."

Oh, I wanted to tell her, but I couldn't have her worrying over me. It would put her life on hold and she had already been accepted at Harvard. No, I was not going to let this be a worry for her as well. "I think I have just been over stressed, but I don't think that not working is helping. I need to just concentrate on the next few weeks, get school over with, and then, maybe then, take a vacation or something. Maybe a road trip before we head off to college."

She smiled. "I like road trips. So where we going?"

"Ladies, I am trying to close up." Ms. Julie stood behind us.

"Sorry, Ms. Julie." I grabbed my books and we headed for Beth's car.

Beth always loved getting out and driving. It really didn't matter where, just the mention of a road trip and she couldn't be happier. We talked all the way home about the possibility of going to New York or Florida. At least I had gotten her off the subject of me. When we stopped in front of the house, I grabbed my books and opened the door to get out when I thought about Matthias.

"Do you mind if Matthias catches a ride with us tomorrow? Mrs. Hawthorne stuck us on a paper together, so he is going to come over and work on it tomorrow after school."

"Lucky you," she said and gave me a big smile. "That's fine. Oh yeah, just to give you a heads up, Sarah hasn't stopped talking about him since lunch." Beth rolled the window down as I shut the door.

"Yeah, I got the impression at lunch that she had laid claim to him already." We both laughed.

"You think she's got a shot at him?" she asked.

"No! He didn't seem too interested in anything but getting away from her once she started throwing herself at him."

"Well, at least he's got that going for him." We both laughed as she drove off.

Chapter 4

Discoveries

Another night of homework? No! I needed a break. I grabbed my running shoes and headed for the park. I needed to run off some stress. The weather was great for early April. It was warm enough not to need a jacket, but cool enough at night to snuggle up in a blanket. Just perfect. I ran down two blocks and over four more to the park. There were lots of people out today. Spring always brought out all the lovebirds. There were couples sitting on blankets, benches, just everywhere. I always knew who was really going to make it as a couple. I stopped by a tree to stretch my legs out a little. The couple sitting closest to me was going to make it; their aura was purple, which meant they were truly in love. But the couple on the bench, well, their colors were still blue and pink, bright blue and bright pink, which meant they were really happy but not in true love. I hoped they figured it out before they did something like get married and have kids. I noticed several purple spots in the park, but most of the couples weren't. Sad, really. I guess that's why divorce was so high. People just seem to be settling on short-term happiness instead of really waiting on the right person to come along.

I circled the park twice. Man, it felt good to get out of the house. On the third lap, a glimmer of silver in a sea of blues caught my eye. It had to be Matthias. He was the only silver I knew of. As I got closer, I noticed there were two silvers, not just one. Matthias I recognized, but the other, well, it had to be his brother since they looked so much alike. Both of them had long black hair and coppery skin. I still had no clue why Matthias was silver, but now there were two of them. His brother appeared much taller, but they looked a lot alike. Wow, they were a sight. They were playing basketball, both on the "skins" team. No shirts! I got so lost in watching them, I forgot to watch where I was going until I hit the ground, face first.

"Are you okay?" I heard a woman ask as I rolled over. I just laughed. I had just plowed over a fire hydrant. The same one I had passed two times already.

"Lindsey?" I heard his voice, no mistaking it. Great, I had just made a complete idiot out of myself. I opened my eyes to find a woman, Matthias, and his brother leaning over me.

"Yeah," I said.

"Here, let me help you up." Matthias held out his hand. I took it and he pulled me up. "What happened?" he asked.

"Stupid fire hydrant just ran right out in front of me." I know my face had to be four shades of red.

"You hurt?" he asked.

"Only my pride."

He smiled. "Hey, this is my brother, Daniel." Daniel stuck out his hand.

"Nice to meet you." I said as I shook his hand.

"Hey, you two!" someone yelled from over at the courts. "You guys coming?"

Matthias looked over at Daniel. "You go ahead. I think I should make sure she gets home okay. You know, watch out for those rogue fire hydrants."

Daniel just smiled. "Yeah, okay." With that, Daniel headed back to the courts.

"You're sure you're okay, sweetie?" the lady asked.

"Yes, I'm fine. Thank you."

"I'll make sure she gets home," Matthias told the lady.

"I can make it home on my own."

"Yeah, I know. So which way is home?" He looked around.

"Seriously, I'm fine."

"Well, that goose egg on your head says maybe or maybe not."

I reached up and felt my forehead. Great, something for Dad to worry about. At least he was working overtime, so I would be in bed before he got home and out before him in the morning. Ouch. I could feel it pulsing now; it sort of made me light-headed for a second. I reached out and took a hold of Matthias' arm to steady myself. He slid his arm around my waist and pulled me close. "I thought so. Your head bounced off the concrete pretty hard. You might have a slight concussion."

I could feel his bare chest against my arm. It was rock solid but smooth to the touch. Lindsey, what are you doing? I thought to myself. Boys don't bother you. Yeah, but he's not normal, was all that came back. "I live on the south side."

"Alright, let's get you home, then."

""Thanks again," I told the lady as we walked past her. She smiled as Matthias led me off.

"I hope you're okay," she called.

I smiled back at her. "I am." I figured we would be heading to a car or something, but we walked across the park and out to the street.

"Which way?" he said. I pointed, and we headed toward home. He still held me close, but I was walking on my own. "So what had you so distracted that you ran over the fire hydrant you had made it by twice already?"

He had noticed me running. I smiled. "Well, it's really silly and embarrassing." I dropped my head.

"All right then, if it was that embarrassing I guess I better let it slide."

Whew, I really did not want to tell him that it was him that distracted me, that copper chest, his long black ... Lindsey! Pull yourself together. I shuttered.

"You okay?"

"Yeah, just still reeling in the stupidity of it." We were on my block now. "Third house on the left." He loosened up his grip a little. We walked to the door. I bent over to get my key out of my shoe. I suddenly felt cold; somewhere in the distance I could hear my name. It sounded soft and smooth. *"Come on, let me help you. Open up to me,"* the voice said. I felt a strange warmth come over me.

"Lindsey? Lindsey?" Something cold and wet was on my face. I opened my eyes to find myself lying on the couch with a cold washcloth on my face and Matthias kneeling beside me. "You passed out on me. Maybe you should go to the hospital."

"No, no. I am fine." I bolted upright so fast that our faces touched. I froze, our checks were together. His face was so soft and warm and ... You're doing it again, Lindsey.

He slowly turned his face so his eyes were looking into mine. His eyes were *mesmerizing*, and our lips were so close I could feel his breath on mine.

He smelled so good, like the forest after a heavy rain. "Anything else I can do for you?" His voice was so soft and gentle, my heart went crazy.

Get a grip, Lindsey, I kept repeating over and over in my head. I leaned back a little. "N-No." I stumbled over the word. He smiled and pulled away.

"You sure you're going to be okay? If you have a concussion, you're not supposed to sleep for a while. Maybe you should give me your number so I can call and check on you every hour." I handed over my phone without hesitating. He handed it back after a couple of minutes. "I put mine in there so you'll know it's me calling."

"Okay." I still wasn't good at talking.

He stood up and walked to the door, paused, and turned around. "I'll see you tomorrow." He turned and left.

My heart was still pounding. What was wrong with me? I didn't go crazy over guys. Sure, I thought he was cute, but there were a lot of guys I thought were cute. They had never had affected me like this, though. I got up slowly just in case. I seemed to be fine, so I headed for my room. Some homework; maybe that would get him out of my head. I spent twenty minutes trying to write one paragraph. It was no use. I still could feel his check on mine, his breath on my face. My heart wouldn't stop racing. Okay, maybe a shower would do the trick. Something had to work. I stood in the shower and let the water just pour over me. His eyes burned in my very soul; every time I closed my eyes they were there so close, looking deep into my soul. Finally, I got out and lay on my bed. I put my headphones on and let the music consume me. My phone vibrating startled me. I looked down. It was him. Had it been an hour already?

"Hello?"

"How you feeling?" I closed my eyes and his eyes were instantly there before me.

"I'm okay."

"No dizziness or anything?" he asked.

"No. I have been up and down the hall several times, had a shower, and nope, no dizziness, so I am just fine." Why did I add shower? Lame Lindsey, like he wanted to know you had showered.

"So, should I call you in an hour again?"

Yes! my head screamed. "No, I'm fine. I told you that I would be." You could just call! my head yelled.

"I guess I'll see you tomorrow, then. But if you get to feeling bad or dizzy, you call me, okay?"

"I will. Thanks for helping me home. I don't know if I said that when you were here."

"You're welcome. Talk to you tomorrow." And the line went dead. I lay back in my bed and closed my eyes. His eyes filled my head, his smell, and his soft skin so warm. His touch; oh, I wanted him to touch me ...

I was sitting in the car next to Dad and it was dark and rainy. I could hear him sobbing. He was wearing a suit. What had happened? I opened my mouth to ask, but nothing came out. I tried to reached over and touch him, but I couldn't move. All I could do was watch. Nothing I tried to do worked. The car stopped. Where were we? I looked around and saw the cemetery where Mom was buried. Dad got out of the car. I followed, but I wasn't moving. I could see people gathered under the tent ahead of us. Beth was there, along with Todd, Kayla, and a bunch of kids from school. Who died? Dad slowly walked to the front and I could see a picture. My breath caught in my throat. It was my funeral.

Let me in. Let me help you. I could hear the words over and over in my head. I felt so cold all of the sudden, everything went black and started spinning. *Let me help you,* I heard again. The spinning slowed and I could feel warmth from somewhere. I could see a small glimmer of light in the blackness. It would get brighter then fade. The spinning would worsen when the light would fade. My eyes flew open.

It was dark. No, there was a glow around me. I blinked to focus; nothing but darkness. I sat up and took a deep breath. It smelled like the woods after a rain. Matthias! I looked slowly around my room, letting my eyes get used to the darkness. I was alone. The clock said 2 a.m. I laid back. I had to be dreaming, but I could smell him. Could you dream a smell? Does that make sense? I had to admit that I had been thinking of him when I fell asleep, but I wasn't dreaming about him. I was dreaming of the funeral, my funeral. It all came rushing back into my head. Great. There was no way I was going to sleep now. I didn't want to relive any of that dream again.

I got up and tiptoed down to the kitchen for a drink. I got a glass out of the cabinet, filled it with water, and went and stood at the patio door. The moon was shining brightly and it was almost like daytime outside. I looked over the backyard. In the very back by the fence there was a small silvery glimmer of light. I strained to see what it was, but it was in the shadow of the fence. I turned and sat my water on the coffee table. The glow was gone. Had I imagined it? I rubbed my eyes. Maybe I did hit my head harder than I though. I finished my water and headed back to my room. I could hear Dad snoring from the end of the hall. I shut my door, turned on my light, picked up a book, and started working on one of the many reports I had due on Monday.

Chapter 5

Never Before

My alarm clock woke me up with its loud beeping. I was lying in the middle of my bed on my books. My light was still on. I had fallen asleep again. Well, at least this time I had showered before I went to bed so I wouldn't make us late today. I got up and headed to my closet to find something to wear. I needed to wash some clothes; almost everything I had was dirty. The only jeans I had clean were ones I hadn't worn in a year, but they were all that were left. Oh well, they would have to do. Which shirt? There wasn't much of a clean selection of them either. I most definitely had to wash tonight. Dad had only four work shirts, and I hadn't washed in weeks. Oh, yuck! I guess he was wearing the same dirty shirts over and over. Yep, laundry tonight for sure. I grabbed an old blue t-shirt, threw it on, and headed to the bathroom to brush my teeth. I looked up in the mirror as I brushed my teeth. My hair was a jumbled mess. This called for a messy bun today. I pulled my hair up quickly, that would have to do. It was great that messy buns were in, because they were easy and messy. I pushed my bangs over to wash my face. Oh, great! Right in the middle of my forehead was a big purple spot. I felt it, and ouch! It was very sore. I carefully washed my face and pulled my bangs back into place to hide it. I heard Beth pull up out front just as I finished. I grabbed my books, threw on my shoes, and headed out.

"Morning," she said as I opened the car door.

"Hey." I threw my books in the backseat and jumped in. She sped off as I fastened my seatbelt.

"You look tired. Did you not sleep last night?" she asked as we turned the corner.

"I had weird dreams last night, so I didn't sleep very good or very long."

"Well, what were they about?"

"I dreamed about riding with Dad to the cemetery. He was really upset like she had just died again." I left out the part about it being my funeral and waking to a glowing room. I didn't want her to worry.

"What do you think it means?" she asked as we pulled into the parking lot.

"That I am so stressed out I am having nightmares."

She smiled at me. "Anything I can do?"

"Nothing, unless you can speed up time so we can graduate." We grabbed our books and headed toward the school.

"Sorry, Lindz. I wish I could."

We got to first period and were in our seats long before the bell rang. First period went by slowly. Ms. Jenkins' lecture seemed to go on and on, but finally the bell rang and I headed to second. Matthias was already waiting for me in study hall.

"Hey, how's the head?" he asked, even before I set my books down. I glanced around, then slid my bangs up for a second and quickly back down. "Well, it looks a lot better than it did yesterday."

I smiled. "It doesn't hurt, well, unless you touch it." He laughed, and the bell rang. I sat down, got my book out, and opened to chapter twenty-four. He did the same. His seat was really close to mine today I noticed. He was so close I could smell him. He smelled so good. It was the same smell from last night. My head started wondering. *"Let me help you."* I could hear the voice again. I could feel his arm touching mine. I looked over at Matthias. I could see his mouth moving, but I couldn't tell what he was saying. *"Please let me in, Lindsey. I need to help you."*

"Why?" I asked the voice. Suddenly, I was aware of Matthias looking at me, his eyes wide. His eyes were amazing, he was totally focused on me, and I met his gaze. Time froze.

The bell suddenly was ringing, and I blinked. Matthias was putting his books away. What happened? Class had just started, and now the bell was ringing. I looked up as he stood. He glanced my way, but kept moving. Something was different. What had happened? Did I do something? Had I said something? I couldn't remember saying anything. All that I could remember was looking into his eyes.

"Are you coming or are you going to stay here through lunch?" He was standing there looking at me, but it was different; it didn't feel the same.

"I'm coming." I gathered up my books. *Feel the same.* How had it felt? How did he feel to me? My mind wandered. He was warm, calming, and gentle, like a breeze blowing through the trees. I walked by him, but really wasn't paying attention to anything around me. Suddenly, his hand was on my waist pulling me back. I blinked. I had almost walked directly into an open door. "Thanks."

"Where are you? It's clear you're not here." I looked up at him. "You need to get your head out of the clouds and back in the game before you walk out in front of a truck or something," he growled at me. Anger. I wasn't expecting that, not from him. I felt a tear roll down my cheek.

What was going on? Why did I all of the sudden want to just lie down and cry like a baby? I had to get out, get away from him before I lost it. I turned so fast my books fell out of my hands. I didn't care; I just left them and took off down the hall. I turned and ran up the stairs through the old chem lab, out and onto my ledge. Tears were rolling down my face. What was wrong with me? Had the cancer finally kicked in? I didn't feel physically sick, just emotionally sick. Emotions. I didn't do emotions, so why were they going crazy now? A tissue came over my shoulder.

"Sorry, Lindsey. I didn't mean to upset you."

Oh, crap! I forgot I had showed him my hiding spot. Matthias slid out on the ledge beside me. He took the tissue and rubbed the tears from my eyes. I couldn't quit crying. He slid over until we were touching. He gently put his arm around me. I turned and looked at him. "I ... I ..." I was trying to say sorry, but I was just stumbling. He put his finger up and touched my lips.

"Shh, just let it all out. No one is here but me and you." His gaze went from my eyes to my lips where his finger rested. His hand gently cupped my chin and his thumb traced my lips. I couldn't breathe. Our eyes met again. He leaned in toward me as if he was going to kiss me, but then he let go and slid away from me. "I ... I am sorry," he stammered. "I don't know what came over me." He started climbing back through the window.

I didn't want him to go. I reached for his arm. "Please don't leave." He didn't move for a moment, but then slowly sat back down.

"Are you sure?" he asked, but he didn't look at me. I took my hand and lifted his chin and turned his head to look at me. Man, I have never wanted to kiss or be kissed by anyone in all my life as much as right then. I let go of his chin and looked away.

"This is insane." I took a deep breath.

He chuckled. "So it's not just me."

I looked back at him. "No." He smiled at me, I smiled back. The tears were gone and forgotten, just that quickly. "I really don't know what is going on with me these days." I took a breath. "The last three weeks have been crazy and evidently, they are playing havoc with my emotions. And then you came along and ..." I looked down. His hand was lying on his leg. He opened it. I placed mine in it and looked up at him. He smiled as he entwined our fingers.

"Tell me. What's been so crazy about the last three weeks, besides me?"

Did I really want to tell him? I hadn't even told Beth. What was it about him that just made me want to show and tell him things that I hadn't even shown or told Beth? No, I couldn't tell him this, not yet. "I don't know if I am really ready to talk about it, not yet anyway." I looked at our fingers, they felt so good together.

"Okay, no pressure. I'm sorry about earlier. I didn't mean to jump down your throat." I glanced up at him. He was looking at our hands, too. "It was really me I was mad at, but I took it out on you. I'm sorry, but it wasn't the first time you hurt yourself on account of me, well almost hurt yourself."

Crap! He did know I was watching him in the park yesterday. What was up with me? Why did I even care? I looked down at our fingers entwined together. This was ridiculous. What was going on? I had just met him three days ago. How in the world could you fall for someone in three days? I didn't know anything about him, well, except he sparkled and glowed silver.

"What?" He was suddenly looking at me.

"Nothing," I sort of laughed. He raised his left eyebrow. "I was just wondering if I was dreaming."

"No, I don't think so," he said without hesitation. "I don't dream." He let go of my hand and climbed back though the window. "We better go down to lunch. Sarah may be getting a search party ready to send out to look for us." I laughed as I climbed back through, too.

As we entered the lunchroom, I saw our books piled on the table with everyone else's. He slid out a chair for me. "You hungry?" he asked as I sat down. "What do you want? I'll go grab it."

"Just an apple and some milk." I smiled.

"No problem. I'll be right back." Suddenly I had a weird feeling. I turned to find everybody at the table was staring at me. Sarah's look was priceless, and it was obvious she wasn't happy.

"Well, well." Kayla was first. "When did this occur?" she asked.

"What?" I said.

"We are not blind or stupid, Lindsey."

Matthias sat the apple and milk in front of me and pulled up a chair beside me. "Did I interrupt something?" Sarah got up and left.

"Ooh," Todd said then laughed. "I would steer clear of her for a while, Lindsey." I just shook my head and took a deep breath.

Matthias looked at me. "Did I miss something?"

"Oh, don't worry about her. She'll get over it," Kayla piped in. I picked up my apple and took a bite. "Well, I am still waiting?" Kayla was staring me down.

Matthias finally got that she was asking about us. He smiled. "I think it was when the fire hydrant ran out in front of her." We both laughed. Of course, everyone at the table looked at us like we were insane. I pulled my bangs back to show them the big purple circle on my forehead.

"I made a complete idiot out of myself yesterday," I said. Todd wanted all the details and Matthias was more than happy to tell them about me running over the hydrant in the park and him having to walk me home. I was glad he left out a few minor details. My heart started beating wildly at just the thought of our cheeks touching and him being so close. Todd's laughing brought me back to reality. I know I must have turned three shades of red then.

"Well, it's about time someone got her attention. Most of the guys were starting to wonder about her." I looked at Kayla. "You have turned down every guy that has ever asked you out," she said.

She was right, I had. I had never been interested in any guy, not until now anyway. I looked at Matthias. He smiled at me. He touched my leg with his hand under the table. A small fire seemed to light in my very soul the instant he touched me. My eyes closed as wave of heat rushed through my entire body as the bell rang. What just happened? I really felt weird for a second. Everyone started leaving, and I looked up to see Matthias still looking at me. I smiled and grabbed my books. He was right behind me as I went out the lunchroom doors.

Chapter 6

Healing in Color

The rest of the day flew by. Beth was mad that I hadn't told her about the park. But when Matthias came up behind me to catch a ride, she quickly changed back into her cheery self. "So what brought you to Chicago, Matthias?" Here she goes, I thought, with her thousand and one questions. I almost laughed out loud. I better pay attention; I didn't know much about him myself.

"My brother. His job takes him all over the world." Beth was driving rather slowly, but the school wasn't far from the house. I could have walked it easily, but it was "Beth and me" time, and there hadn't been a lot of that lately.

"What does he do?" she asked.

"He restores old houses."

She pulled up in front of the house. "That's cool." I opened the door and got out. Matthias followed.

"Thanks for the ride, Beth."

She smiled. "Anytime."" She gave me one of her go-for-it smiles and drove off.

I dropped all my books on the table as we went in, and then flopped down on the couch. He just stood there looking at me. He almost looked nervous. I got up, took his books, and laid them on the table with mine. "Have a seat," I told him as I dropped back on the couch. He sat down. "You want a drink or anything?" I got up and headed into the kitchen for some water.

"No, thanks. I'm fine." He just watched me. I got a bottle out of the fridge and sat back down on the couch beside him. "We should probably get started." He got up and retrieved our books from the table.

"Oh, come on. Let's take a breather from schoolwork for a minute." He slowly sat the books back down, made his way back to the couch, and sat down beside me. Our legs touched. Heat suddenly flickered within me. I looked at him. He looked as nervous as I felt all of the sudden. "You okay?" I asked.

As he turned toward me, his eyes said it all. They were the largest I had ever seen them; they swirled with emotions. I got caught in them in a split second. *"Oh Lindsey,"* I heard the voice in my head. *"Why is it so hard for me to help you? Why do you affect me so?"*

Was his the voice I kept hearing? I looked deep into his eyes. *"Matthias?"* I asked the voice. *"Is that you?"* His eyes got wide. He drew back from me and blinked. "It is you. How are you doing that?" I asked him out loud.

He looked down a second and then back up. Matthias' *"What?"* echoed in my head.

"How are you in my head?" I didn't say it out loud. He didn't answer *"Matthias!"* I yelled in my head.

"I don't know how to explain it." He spoke out loud this time. He was looking down again. I reached over to lift his head, but he pulled away. My hand dropped. He finally lifted his head and looked at me. "Okay, since I can't seem to reach you any other way, here goes." He took a deep breath. "Well ... I really don't know how to tell you or even start to explain to you what I do." I took his hand in mine. He looked down at what I was doing. He closed his eyes and took another deep breath. "I need you to let me do something. I can't explain, but I might be able to show you. Just close your eyes."

"Show me? What do you mean, 'show me'?"

"Please, Lindsey, just close your eyes." I took a deep breath and closed them. There was a glimmer of light in the distance. It got brighter until a young woman appeared. She was lying in her bed. You could see she was sick from all the medicine bottles and stuff in her room. It sort of reminded me of how Mom looked right before she died. She was glowing bright yellow. As the woman lay there asleep, a sudden silver glow appeared over her. It was Matthias. He was floating in the air just above her. The yellow emanating from her started to rise. It completely covered Matthias for a few seconds, then it just disappeared. She was now pink again. Matthias then vanished. In the next scene that appeared before my eyes, the lady was cutting flowers in her garden. She now looked healthy and happy. More scenes came and went, depicting lots of sick and dying people. Each time he hovered above them, they became well. The scenes finally stopped and the light faded away. I opened my eyes. I was still sitting on the couch. I looked at Matthias. He looked over at me.

"Did I just dream that?"

"No," he answered. I didn't know whether to be scared or just freaked out. Had he just healed all those people? How could he do that?

"Are you human?" I finally got out, after trying several times.

"Yes, I just have a few added bonuses," he answered. "Can I ask you something?" He looked at me. "What were the colors around everyone I showed you? I have never seen them before." The question took me aback. I never thought about it being strange to him. Wait. Wasn't *he* showing *me* things? How did he see my colors? I must have had a strange look on my face or he was reading my mind, because he answered my question. "I was watching through you, so I could see if you were seeing it or not."

Seeing through me, wow. How could he do that? I couldn't figure it out. Oh, the colors. He wanted to know about the colors. "I see people differently than most. I see people's auras." He looked at me with wide eyes. "The lady you showed me first, she was yellow, which meant she was dying. Did you notice how she turned pink? Pink is health. Now, guys turn brown when they are dying."

"So, blue means they are healthy?" He was catching on.

"Yes," I answered.

"Are there any other colors?"

"Well, yes. Girls turn orange when they are getting sick and guys, green. But of course the colors get lighter or darker depending on the intensity of their moods. The only other color I had ever seen was purple. When two people are meant for each other and they stand together, well, they both turn purple."

"You said, 'had seen.'"

"That's because you are silver, like a bunch of shiny diamonds stuck together. I didn't know there were any other colors until I saw you." Okay, that was enough about colors. I wanted to know more about him. "So, you heal people, right?" He shook his head. This was great! He had to be here to heal me. "So are you here to heal my cancer?"

He looked surprised. "So that's what you have!" Okay, that took me aback. I figured he knew that already.

"You mean you didn't know?"

He smiled at me. "You seem to be a little different than anyone else I have ever healed. For some reason, I can't seem to just get into you, so to speak. I have been having a lot of trouble trying to find out what needed healed. You have to understand that I have never had to reveal myself before. But since I could find no other way, I decided to show you how I heal others so that maybe you would let me in to help you."

Different, that was me alright. Did he just say he couldn't heal me? He answered my thought. "No, that's not what I said. I said I had to have your permission or something like that. Just like I had to ask you to let me show you things, I think I have to ask for your permission to even seek your cancer." I had to wonder if he could find it at all. Find the dreaded cancer I had but didn't have. "What do you mean you have but don't have?" he asked.

"Can I show you things like you showed me?"

He looked over at me. "Yes, that's the way it usually works."

"It would be easier to show you rather than trying to explain the last few weeks." I was glad our fingers were still together; this was sort of scary. *"Can you hear me?"* I asked in my head.

"Yes," came his voice. *"Open your mind, Lindsey, and show me."* I let my mind wander back to the first day in Doc Harvey's office. Him telling me I had cancer and the near hopelessness that threatened to consume me. The dreams of Mom and her death were next, then to the sense of fear of hurting Dad again. Then Doc Jenkins and Mary in Lexington, and all the new information about having cancer but it not hurting me yet. All the way until the day he walked into the office and I was staring at his glow.

One thing I noticed in my mind that I hadn't remembered was Mary and Dr. Jenkins' glow. Blue and pink, but oh, so bright purple when they stood close together. I opened my eyes. Matthias' face was inches from mine. His eyes looked into mine. His hand touched my face. My eyes closed and my heart started racing. I could hear the echo of it in his head. His hand slid down my jaw. *"Oh, just kiss me, please,"* I thought. His hand froze. *"Oh, crap! This mind thing sucks."*

"I have never kissed anyone before," he said in my head. He was still close to me, still looking at me.

"That makes two of us," I whispered. He almost looked scared as he stood up and backed away from me. I stood up and stepped close to him. He took a deep breath.

"I have never felt ... well, I have never felt anything before now, before you." My heart started to race again. I reached out for him, but he suddenly vanished. I stood there alone. What just happened? The room started spinning. I felt his hands on my waist, and the spinning slowed. I blinked to focus. He was standing in front of me again. He pulled me against him until our faces were inches apart. "You have the strangest effect on me." I pushed up on to my tiptoes until our lips were almost together. He was still, not a single movement. Then the gap closed, his lips were on mine. They were soft and smooth, and my hands slid up into his hair. The fire lit in my soul again, like it had at lunch. Our bodies pressed tightly together.

A noise grabbed my attention. Matthias disappeared and I was left standing there alone again. My body shuddered with the heat surging through it. I fell back on the couch. I heard the noise again. It was Dad's keys in the front door. Dad was home. I started to panic. We hadn't done anything. I looked around; our books were spread out on the floor, notebooks open. Several ripped out papers lay on the floor. How had he done that? Where was he? I would have to ask later. I slid down onto the floor as the door opened. My head was spinning again. Get a grip, Lindz, I kept telling myself over and over. "Hey, Dad." The toilet flushed in the background. So that's where he was. I could hear the water running in the sink. "How was work?" I leaned back on the couch. Heart, stop racing, I told myself again.

"Not bad. Looks like you have been working all afternoon here," he said as he stepped over a book.

"Got a report due on Monday, Mrs. Hawthorne's class. She did assign me a partner, so it is not as bad as it could have been." Matthias stepped into the living room. "Dad, this is Matthias, the partner Mrs. Hawthorne paired me with."

Matthias stepped forward and stuck out his hand. "Nice to meet you, sir."

Dad shook his hand. "You can call me Matt."

Dad smiled at him. "Matthias. I haven't heard that name in a long time."

"Yeah, it's from the Bible. My dad was a missionary."

Dad smiled. "So, what did you guys have for supper? I am starved."

Until that point, I hadn't even thought of food. What time was it? It had to be after eight since Dad was home. "Oh my, I guess I got so wrapped up in the work that I hadn't even thought of food. Matthias may be starving." I turned to look at him, standing there so calm and relaxed.

"No, I am fine. Matter of fact, I better be getting home before my brother starts calling me every fifteen minutes or so. If I am not home by nine, he gets all mother hen on me." He turned to look at me. "So when do you want to work on this some more?"

I looked at Dad. "Are we hiking this weekend or are you working?"

He sighed. "I am working all day tomorrow and working the late shift Sunday." We hadn't seen much of each other since we got home from Kentucky. Normally, we spent one day every weekend doing something together and the other I usually spent with Beth, but nothing seem to be normal anymore.

"Well, that's okay. Then I won't feel bad about working on my report and not spending time with you. And Beth is dying to go see the new Brad Pitt movie." I smiled at Dad.

""Well good. Looks like there was going to be no time for hiking anyway."

I turned back to Matthias. "What about tomorrow around 10 a.m., unless you have plans?"

"No, that's good. I guess I will see you tomorrow." He knelt down and started picking up our books.

"Just leave them. You will back in the morning."

He looked around the room. "I hate to leave such a mess." I glanced up at Dad. He was smiling, too.

"Oh, don't worry about it. It was nice to meet you, Matthias."

He looked up at Dad. "You too, sir. Goodnight." He smiled at me then headed out the door.

"Seems like a nice guy. I thought I knew all your friends?" Dad turned to look at me.

"He's new. Today was his third day at school." I headed for the kitchen. "I'll get us something to eat." My mind wandered as I put some chicken on to grill and made us a salad. Matthias was here to heal me. But how could he be here to heal me and not know I had cancer? Well, I wasn't sure I had it or not myself. And then there was the vanishing thing. What else could he do? Human with bonuses, he had said. How could you be human and vanish, and what about the books and notes? How did he do that? There was also the whole kissing thing. Was that one of the bonuses he was talking about? My mind spun with questions. I played the whole evening over and over again looking for answers, but didn't find any.

Dad sat the table as I pulled the chicken off the grill. His shirt looked horrible. "I'll wash clothes tomorrow, Dad. Sorry I hadn't already," I told him as we sat down to eat.

"That's okay, Lindz. I know you're busy trying to catch up with your schoolwork." He looked at me. The truth was that neither one of us thought I would be here long enough to finish the year out. Sad, really. I had made all the plans on how to live and do things normally, but had not given school a thought. "So, Matthias seems like a nice guy."

I smiled at Dad. If only he knew. "Yeah, I think he's one of the good guys."

Dad laughed. "Not too many of those left these days, are there?"

I laughed. "Nope, not many at all."

Chapter 7

Nightmares

I lay on my bed, thinking about the day. I still wasn't sure what had happened. Maybe I was dreaming. I closed my eyes. His lips were so soft and I wanted to feel them again, wanted his arms around me ...

It was dark. I was running though a large meadow. I could hear an awful sound coming from behind me. Not really close, but it was gaining. The sound was getting closer with every passing second. I glanced over my shoulder. I could see a red glow coming from the edge of the meadow as I ran. I was running as hard as I could, heading for the other edge. The noise was getting extremely loud now. It sounded like a thousand people all screaming in horror at once. Whatever it was, it was about to catch me. I wasn't going to make it. I stopped and turned to face it. A flash of silver came between me and the red glow. In the red glow was a large creature that looked like something from a horror movie. It reached for the silver. No ...

"Lindsey, I need to help you. Let me in," a voice echoed in my head. *"Let me help you, please,"* the voice pleaded. The scene before me started fading away. It grew dark and cold. *"I have to help you."* A small glimmer of light appeared in the distance. *"Relax and open yourself to me."* The light started getting brighter. I started to feel warm.

"Matthias ..."

"Just sleep, Lindsey."

The light was very bright, but now it was the sun. I was walking through the forest and the sun was shining through the trees. It must have just rained. I could smell the fresh smell it always brought with it. I walked on and on. It was so peaceful there. I found a large rock and laid down on it in the sun. It felt so warm and good. The day melted into the most beautiful sunset I had ever seen. The night sky was clear and the moon was full. The breeze blew across my face. It was cool, but I wasn't cool at all. I looked down to see that I was wrapped in a silver flowing blanket. *"Matthias …"* My eyes opened. He was inches from me, floating in the air. He slowly opened his eyes to look into mine. His eyes were wide. I wanted to reach up and touch him. His hand was touching my face. He hovered just above me, but seemed to be getting closer. I could smell him. I could almost feel his body he was so close. My heart took off and was racing at high speed. Flames were starting to grow. I felt light as air. My body molded itself against his. *"What are you doing to me?"* My body was burning in flames. He looked surprised. It felt like we were rising in the air. I closed my eyes.

Suddenly I was wet and cold. My eyes flew open. I was lying on my bed drenched in sweat, and alone. Had I been dreaming? I got up and went into the bathroom. I looked in the mirror. My hair was even damp. I slid out of my clothes and into the shower. The water felt good. Was it all a dream or had he really been here? I washed and then put a towel around me and headed back to my room. My phone lay on my nightstand. Should I? I sat down on the edge of the bed and picked it up. I scrolled down to his name.

"Hello?" His voice was smooth and gentle.

"Did I wake you?" I asked.

"No." His voice didn't come from the phone but from behind me. I turned to find him sitting on the bed. I closed the phone. I suddenly was aware I was still in my towel. "Do you need something?" he asked. I looked up at him. All he had on was a pair of shorts, so his chest was bare. My mind fluttered back to the day I saw him playing ball in the park. "Lindsey, focus. What do you want?"

My eyes struggled to get past his chest to his eyes. "I just wanted to know if you were here about thirty minutes ago or did I dream it?"

He reached up and ran his finger across my cheek and down my jaw line. He suddenly pulled it back quickly, as if he had been burned. He closed his eyes for a second then opened them to look at me. "Thirty minutes ago? No, I have been looking for Daniel all night." He looked down. "I can't find him."

He couldn't find his brother. Was that bad? "What do you mean, 'can't find him'?"

He looked back up. "You have to understand, we can find anyone instantly by thinking of them. It works the same for each other. But for some reason, I can't find him."

I reached out and touched his arm. "Do you think something has happened to him?" I slid my hand down into his.

"I don't know." He looked down to our hands. He was definitely bothered by not being able to find his brother. I slid over on the bed beside him. His hair was hanging down around his face. He was so handsome. He looked up at me. Fear! Was that fear I saw in his eyes? "I have got to find him."

"Is there anything I can do to help?" I knew that there was nothing I could do, but I had to ask.

His eyes suddenly flashed. "He's back. I have to go." He vanished.

I wondered what was going on. And until that point, I hadn't really thought about his brother at all. Daniel. I had met him in the park and he was as silver as Matthias. But did that mean he could do things like him? He must. Matthias had just said *they* could find anyone instantly, so it had to mean his brother was like him. So who was his brother here healing? More things to think about. I got up, put my pj's on, and lay back down. My nightmare flashed through my mind. I guess I was entitled to a few, with all the things I had been through lately. But the voice. It had sure seemed real, and I was sure that I felt him against me there for a second or two. I closed my eyes. I guessed it was all a dream. Matthias was to blame for the second part of my dream, but at least it was sort of pleasant. Well, it could have gotten better if I hadn't woken up. I laughed. I guess he really hadn't been here after all, but it sure had seemed so real. Maybe that was just because I would have sure liked for it to have been real.

Chapter 8

Light my Fire

The sun was gleaming through my window when I woke. I rolled over and looked up at the clock. 9:30 a.m. Oh my gosh! I sat up. Matthias was supposed to be here at 10. I jumped up and went to the closet. Crap, I hadn't done laundry. I went to the bathroom and sorted out the clothes and loaded the washer. 9:55 and I was still in my pj's.

"Morning," I heard as I came into the living room. There he stood in the doorway like he had been there all morning. His hair hung half over his shoulder and half in the front, his white t-shirt making his black hair look almost like it had blue in it. Man, he was handsome.

"Is everything okay with Daniel?"

He walked over and sat down on the couch. "Yeah, he's fine. He just got called. He didn't have time to tell me before he had to leave, so he came back just a few minutes when he could to tell me."

"Was anything wrong?"

Matthias laughed. "I don't mean a phone call."

"What other call is there?"

Matthias smiled at me again. "I know you won't understand, but I really don't know how to explain it to you. What made me worry is that we have never been called separately. But I guess there is a first time for everything."

I walked over and stood in front of him. "So everything is okay?"

"He didn't say. He just came back to tell me he'd been called as a protector, so he would see me well ... when he saw me." I flopped down on the couch and crossed my legs facing him. Called as a protector, what

53

was that? Who does the calling? My head spun with all kinds of questions. "He didn't stay but just a second. He just didn't want me to worry about him." He lifted his hand and a notebook appeared in his hand. "I finished the report last night. You can look over it if you want." He handed me the notebook.

"Didn't you get any sleep?" I said as I took it.

"Nope, I don't sleep."

"Ever?" I asked.

"No, never. Well, not in ..." He smiled. "You know, if I counted birthdays like you, I would be over one hundred and seventy years old. But I am just twenty, well, eighteen for this spot in time so that I could get back into school."

I was dumbfounded. One hundred and seventy. I was only eighteen and had just begun to live. He had lived a hundred and seventy years. I was still holding the notebook, but I wasn't really interested in it, so I closed it and sat it on the coffee table. "I'll look at it later." He was a lot more interesting than some paper. "So what do you do all night if you don't sleep?"

"Mainly I do my healing, but when I am not doing that, I read, listen to music. Nighttime is all mine." He smiled. "I guess I like it because I do not have to pretend. I guess it's my 'me' time."

I looked at him. "So you're pretending with me?"

He smiled. "School, things that normal people do, that's the pretending part. I really have no need for those things except to blend in. It makes my job easier." I raised my eyebrow. He took my hand. "Oh, yeah. What did you dream last night that you thought I had been here?"

"See for yourself." I closed my eyes. The dream came flooding back, the running from the creature, the bright light and the voice coming into my head to pull me out of the dream, to him being above me, the closeness, the burning when our bodies molded together, then the sudden falling and being cold and wet in my bed. When I opened my eyes, his were still closed. He just sat there for a moment. He finally opened his eyes and looked at me. I knew he had seen the whole thing. "I guess all the chaos in my life has thrown me into nightmares." He looked over at me as if he was going to say something, but then didn't. "Can you do more than just vanish and heal people?"

He smiled. "I manipulate things." I looked at him. Was he manipulating me? "People have free will to choose what happens to them, so I can't manipulate people."

Whew, that was a relief. My stomach gave a sudden growl. "Do you eat?"

He smiled; he knew what I thinking. "Not really, but you do. Come on." He got up and pulled me up too. "Let's get you some breakfast or lunch, maybe brunch as close to lunch as it is." We went into the kitchen. He opened the fridge. "So what do you like?"

"You cook?" He lifted his head over the fridge door and looked at me.

"Blend in, right?" He smiled at me.

"A veggie omelet sounds good." My stomach growled again.

"Well, that sounds like you need it now, not in fifteen minutes." He closed the door and walked across the floor to where I stood and handed me a plate. On it was the best-smelling omelet I had ever smelled.

"Cheater," I said.

He laughed. "I can do it the other way, if you like." My stomach growled a great big growl. "I guess that means no." I sat down at the table. He handed me a glass of juice and a fork. "Anything else?"

I looked up. "Piece of toast?" He handed it to me, and then sat down across the table from me. I ate and he watched. "Do you smell food?"

He laughed. "Sure I do, I can even tell you what it took to make it, but I have no desire to eat it."

"So you don't eat, you don't sleep. What else do you not do?" I could see him thinking about something.

"Well, until recently I didn't think I felt some emotions. Or maybe I just had never experienced them, I really don't know." I could help you out with that, I thought, and a picture of the two of us kissing went through my head. He smiled. I stuffed a big bite in my mouth and looked down. I was sure my face was red. I finished and started to take the plate to the sink, but it disappeared from my hands.

"How do you do that?"

"No clue, I just know I can."

The washer buzzer sounded. I raised an eyebrow. "Can you ..."

"It's done and put away. All of it." I had clean clothes again.

"I could get used to that."

He smiled. "Maybe you should take advantage of it and put some clothes on." It was going on 11:30 and I was still in my pj's. I headed down the hall. I had to wonder if he dressed or just did that thing. I bet he cheated at everything. Well, I would if I could. "You done yet?" he said from behind me.

"No."

"No, you're not? You're already dressed." I looked down. Jeans and a t-shirt.

"Would you prefer something else?"

He looked at my closet. "No, this is good." I closed my closet doors.

"So what are we doing today if the paper is done?" I asked.

"What would you like to do?" He didn't have to ask twice.

"Get out of the city."

He smiled. "Let's go, then." He ushered me to the door. I now had boots, sunglasses, and a backpack on. I wondered if I would suddenly find myself elsewhere. He smiled and picked up my car keys. "I move things, not people."

"Dad hasn't been letting me drive." I told him.

"I'll drive," he said as he opened the passenger door. I got in, and he we went around and got in the driver's seat. "So where to?" he asked.

"Surprise me." I fastened my seatbelt. His was already on. He backed out of the driveway and headed south. The radio kicked on. Man, that is just sort of freaky.

"Sorry." He reached down and started going through the channels. He was a good driver, but I guess he was probably good at everything; he had years of practice. He stopped the channel on a sort of bluesy-sounding guitar. He smiled as the music played. I just watched him. The music seemed to speak to him. The expressions on his face changed with the music. I had to admit it was great music. My arm lay across the console. He slid his hand into mine. I loved the way his hand felt in mine. The flame in my hand was gentle, but was there the minute he touched me.

We had been on the road just over an hour when we turned down a gravel road and then onto another. We had headed south then west when we left the house so I was sure we were getting close to Starved Rock State Park. Dad and I love hiking and camping there. We passed a sign that read: "Wildlife Preserve – Keep Out – Official Use Only." I looked over as we passed the sign. He just smiled and kept going. The road stopped at a meadow. He got out and had my door open before I could get my hand on the handle. The meadow was long and there had to be a stream close by, since I could hear water running over rocks. But if we were in Starved Rock, I didn't recognize it.

"This is my special spot. I come here at night. There is a rock on the other end of the meadow that I usually find myself sitting on, listening to my iPod. Come on, I'll show you." He took my hand and we headed down the meadow. I looked around. It was beautiful here. It was nice to know he liked the outdoors, too. You just never know, even with Indian blood. I took my hand from his and did a little swirling dance. He laughed. A sudden weird sensation came over me. Had I been here before? Things sort of looked familiar to me. Maybe I had been here before. I must have had a strange look on my face, or he was reading my mind. "Have you been here before?" I started to feel like I was going to have a panic attack. "What is it?"

My mind drifted. It was dark, I was running though a large meadow, and I could hear an awful sound behind me. Not really close, but it was gaining. The sound was getting closer with every passing second. "Lindsey?" My eyes opened. We were in the meadow of my dream. Matthias held me in his arms. He looked down at me. His eyes told me he had seen what I did. He hadn't had to ask. He shook his head.

"What?" I asked as I looked him in the face.

"I have to be touching you. Your eyes closed and you fell back. When I touched you, I could see what you were seeing."

A break through! Finally we knew how it worked. Even with the good news I felt a little nervous about being here where my nightmare had taken place. He was still holding me tight and close. His eyes were so beautiful and dark. A fire started growing in me. He sat my feet on the ground, but was still holding me. Breathing was getting hard. I felt as if I stood in flames. His eyes were swirling. He lowered his lips to mine. Breathe, I kept telling myself. His lips were so soft and smooth. Flames exploded, like the world had caught on fire and was burning out of control. My hands were around his neck. My fingers slid through his hair. Our bodies molded together. I felt as if we were ... above the ground? Our lips parted and we fell. We had been in the air! I looked over at him. He was just as amazed as I was.

"I thought you couldn't move people?"

He looked at me. "I can't, I know I can't. I've tried before and I can't." He got up and pulled me up and to him again. I looked at him and smiled. The flame lit. His lips were on mine. An explosion ensued. We lifted in the air. He slowly backed off the intensity, down to a gentle kiss, and our feet touched the ground. Our lips parted. "It's you. When you burst into flames, we lift." So the flames were just mine. I looked down. He lifted my head. "You're not the only one that fights a fire."

"So why do you say it is me, then?"

He smiled. "Because I kept my flame down that time and you didn't." He grinned. "Again?"

"Oh, yeah." The flame started at "oh yeah" and before our lips could meet, we were already in the air. When they did meet, the flame roared and we were over the meadow. *We are going to be in outer space if you don't calm down.* I backed the flame down, down, down until our feet touched the ground. My heart was still pounding in my ears. I pulled back and took a deep breath. His hand touched my face. He was suddenly a few feet in the air. His hand was the only thing touching me. He dropped it, but he didn't fall. I could feel him. It was strange; it was like I could feel everything around me. I lifted off the ground until our bodies were together; my hands slid up around his neck. His eyes locked with mine. His hands held my waist. We were high above the meadow again. His touch was like liquid fire to me. I closed my eyes and pulled the flames back down until we were on the ground. I had a hard time keeping the flames down as long as he was touching me. I backed away from him. I closed my eyes. I had to get control of myself. I wanted him so badly. I wanted to feel him against me, to feel his hand on me.

"Uh, Lindsey?" I opened my eyes. He was fifty feet in the air, but I was still on the ground. Oh, crap. He dropped, but vanished before he could hit the ground. He reappeared beside me. He was smiling. "You're amazing."

I didn't feel amazing. I felt lost. I had no idea what I was doing. "Sorry."

"For what, being amazing?"

I smiled. "I didn't mean to drop you."

"Don't worry about it. You can't hurt me." All afternoon, he would light the flame and I would try to control it. We only stopped for a few minutes at supper so I could eat. I tried to tell him I wasn't hungry, but it was no use. He kept putting food in my hands. So I finally gave in and sat on his rock and ate. When the sun started going down, we headed for the car. I was glad, I really didn't like the idea of being in the meadow after dark. I stopped him just before we got there.

"One last time."

"Alright," he said.

I closed my eyes, and he lifted into the air. Then I slowly lifted to meet him. Our lips met. It took great concentration to keep us low to the ground, but I finally got us back down while our lips were still together. Success!

Chapter 9

Protector

I lie in bed that night going over the whole day in my head. I drifted off to sleep with a smile ...

It was dark. I was running though a large meadow. I could hear an awful sound coming from behind me. Not really close, but it was gaining. The sound was getting closer every second. I glanced over my shoulder and I could see a red glow coming from the edge of the meadow as I ran. I was running as hard as I could, heading for the other edge. The noise was getting extremely loud now, and whatever it was, it was about to catch me. I wasn't going to make it. I stopped and turned to face it. A flash of silver came between me and the red glow. It reached for the silver. No! I screamed. The creature was holding the man in the silver by his throat. His silver was flickering and turning red ... *"Lindsey, let me in."* The voice echoed in my head. The scene faded away, and it got cold and dark. A small glimmer of silver light started growing in the distance. I started feeling warmer as the light grew stronger.

"Matthias ..."

"Just sleep, Lindsey." I was in the meadow again, but it was bright and sunny. I danced around in the sun. It was warm and wonderful. The sun was going down, the sunset was beautiful, and I was wrapped tightly in my blanket of silver. I opened my eyes to see the silver hovering above me, his hand touching my face again. He opened his eyes. The flames started. I lifted off the bed, but before I got close enough to touch him he vanished. I fell back in the bed. I am not dreaming, I told myself. I reached for my

59

phone and dialed his number. It rang once and he was sitting beside me. "Why did you leave?"

"When?"

"Just now. I opened my eyes and you vanished."

He looked at me. "Show me." I closed my eyes and he laid his hand on my arm. The dream came flooding back—the creature, the meadow, the silver blanket, then my eyes opening and the silver disappearing. I opened my eyes. He just sat there a minute. "That's the same dream from the other night and from the meadow earlier, isn't it?" he asked.

"Yes, but you're not telling me why you left."

His eyes widened. "That wasn't me. It was Daniel!"

Could it have been Daniel? I thought. They did look a lot alike and it was dark. But why was Daniel here?

"You're the one he got called to protect."

"Protect from what? Why would I need protecting?" I asked.

"I am not real sure yet."

My mind wandered. What could I need protection from? Bad dreams! I suddenly remembered the first night I had the nightmare, except I wasn't remembering the scary part, but what followed. Our bodies molding together and me wanting him so badly. Now I knew why he left so quickly this time. He wasn't going to give me the opportunity to assault him again. Suddenly I was aware that Matthias' arm was on mine and he was seeing the first dream and all that followed.

"You're right. I am sure it was why he left so suddenly." He chuckled.

"I thought it was you," I said as I punched him in the arm.

"I haven't seen Daniel since the night you had the first dream."

"So you don't know what he is protecting me from?"

He didn't answer my question. "I do know that if he is protecting you, then he's close by." He looked around as if he would be in the room with us. Maybe he was; I really didn't understand all this. "You better get some sleep. I'll see you in the morning."

I didn't want him to leave. "Stay." I took a hold of his arm. He turned to face me. If Daniel was protecting me like Matthias said and was close by, then it wouldn't hurt if he stayed a bit would it?

"Just until you fall asleep." I stretched out on the bed against his chest and closed my eyes. He smelled so good. He felt so good. "None of that. You're supposed to be going to sleep."

I opened my eyes to find us halfway to the ceiling. "Sorry." We floated back to the bed. I lie there trying to keep my flames at bay. I didn't know if I could do it. But I was going to, because I wanted him to stay!

Chapter 10

Angels and Demons

I woke to the bright sun coming through my window. I could still smell Matthias on my pillow. I turned over and sat up. I could smell eggs. Great, Dad was cooking again. Last time he almost set the house on fire. I headed down the hall and into the kitchen. Dad was sitting at the table and Matthias was at the stove.

Dad smiled. "Hey Lindz."

Matthias dropped two omelets on plates. "Just in time." He turned and set the omelets on the table. I opened the silverware drawer and got out forks. The toaster popped out two pieces of toast.

"Juice or milk, Dad?" I turned and got two glasses out.

"Milk," he answered.

"What are you doing here cooking breakfast?" I asked Matthias as I poured the milk.

"You said to be here at nine to finish the paper, or was I wrong and you meant nine tonight?"

"That doesn't explain why you're cooking breakfast."

He just smiled. "I like to cook, and your dad was hungry." I just shook my head.

"He offered," Dad broke in. I sat down across from and Dad and began to eat. "Are you not going to eat any of this?" Dad asked him.

"No, sir. I get up early every morning and usually have breakfast with my brother before he leaves for work."

"Well that's nice," Dad said and began to eat. Liar, I thought. You don't eat and you haven't seen Daniel in two days. "This is really good. You going to be a chef or something?" Dad asked.

"No, but I like watching the Food Network. You learn all kinds of things on there." Matthias smiled at me then turned and started cleaning up.

"I'll do that." I got up.

"You go on and eat. I don't mind. It will give me something to do while you finish and get dressed."

I hadn't even thought about still being in my pj's. It's not like he hadn't seem me in them last night, but I was sure I was looking real good. I probably had hair sticking out all over. I finished eating in record time and headed for the bathroom. I looked in the mirror. Why they both weren't laughing, I didn't know. I looked horrible. My hair looked like a bird had been trying to make a nest in it or something. I grabbed the brush and worked on getting the mess all out. I washed up and got dressed. By the time I got back, they were both sitting in the living room, Dad in his recliner and Matthias on the couch. Matthias had gotten the books open and made it look like he was working on the paper, even though he had already finished it.

"Well, I will let you guys get that thing finished. I have got to go see James and run a few errands before I go to work." Dad got up and went down the hall.

I dropped on the couch next to Matthias. "Did you talk to Daniel last night?"

"No, but I really didn't expect to. I thought maybe since I knew who he was protecting that he might come talk to me, but he didn't."

I wondered if it bothered him that Daniel wasn't talking to him. "What does it really mean for you to protect someone? I mean, what would you be protecting someone from?"

He sat there for a second. He had said I wouldn't understand when he told me Daniel had been called, but I needed to know now. I needed to understand. "If we are called to protect, it's usually from ... well, supernatural things. Most people have no clue they are being attacked. It's sort of on a spiritual level." I could see he was really having a hard time putting it in layman's terms for me. "Something like that, anyway."

"So I am being attacked?" The thought of being attacked by anything wasn't good, but I figured he was just keeping me from walking out in front of a bus or something, not being attacked by a ... a what? A supernatural being? Well, wasn't that sort of what they were? I really didn't know. They never sleep, don't eat or drink, they can move things, and they appear and disappear. That sounded pretty supernatural to me. He said the people didn't know they were being attacked. How could you be attacked and not know it? "You were right. I really don't understand."

He sat there a minute looking at me. "I need to show you something," he said.

"Alright," I told him and I closed my eyes.

He took my hand; it felt warm. A light started coming into focus. Two people standing near a streambed. I soon recognized the two. It was Matthias and Daniel. They were a vibrant blue color. They were standing over a fire on the ground. No, they weren't just standing there, they were in a frozen state, looking across the stream. A sound was coming from the woods in front of them. It was a horrible sound that I recognized. Something moved. They both watched as a creature came out of the woods. It was large and vibrant red. It was the creature from my dreams, but now facing it through a different dream, I could get a good look at it. It looked like a man, but then again, it didn't. It stood tall, yet slouched low. Its eyes were as red as its aura. Matthias and Daniel were both in a defensive crouch. The creature attacked them; there was no hope for either of them. The creature fed on them. I wanted to turn away, but couldn't move. Another sound came from the woods, but I didn't recognize this one. The creature dropped the boys and fled into the woods as if scared.

Silver light was coming from the woods. It was too bright to make out a figure; you really couldn't look directly at it. It hovered over the boys, who were squirming in pain on the ground. The color around the boys had turned brown they were dying. They got still and the color around them left. Their lifeless bodies lifted up and hung in the air. A small spark of color started coming from them. It was red. The silver being held them there in the air until they were as bright red as the creature. "Choose," boomed through the air. It was like thunder. One of the boys turned silver and was healed from all the wounds the creature had inflicted. The other struggled in the air for only a minute then turned silver, too. They were both lowered to the ground. They both fell immediately prostrate on the ground in front of the being. "Go," thundered through the air and they vanished. The scene disappeared as well.

I sat there wondering what it was he had just shown me. It couldn't be a dream. He didn't sleep. So what was it? "Do you dream?" I asked Matthias.

He looked at me strangely. "No."

"Then what was that a vision from?"

He understood now. "That was the day Daniel and I became ... well, what we are today. What I really don't know or understand is what is happening to you. I mean, I thought I was here to heal you, but now Daniel's protecting you and you're seeing the demon ..."

"Demon? That creature was a demon?" I was in sudden shock. "So who was the other being, the bright light?"

He looked at me and smiled. "He was an angel, actually *the* angel, The Angel that answers only to the Most High whose name cannot be spoken among men." Okay. I was seeing demons and angels. No, not just any angel, the angel that answered to ... My head started to spin. Matthias took my face in his hands. "Focus, Lindsey." He held my face close to his. I blinked a couple of times. If the other silver was an angel, was he an angel? "Sort of, I guess," he answered my thought. "I am not like him who made me. He was divine and I ... well, I am still human." He was staring deep into my eyes. Oh, he had such amazing eyes. He was so good looking, how in the world had I gotten lucky enough to have an angel looking out for me? He rubbed down my jaw line with his finger. Suddenly he dropped his hand and sat back. "What was the name of the author of that book, *Evolution: A Scientific Fact?*"

Dad came into the living room. "Well, I am heading to the garage to check with James about the mower. I can't keep borrowing Fred's again this summer. Then I am heading to work."

I hopped up and gave him a kiss on the cheek. "Okay, have a good day, Dad."

"Thanks again for breakfast, Matthias. It was really good."

"You're welcome, sir." Dad smiled at him, gave me a kiss back, and headed out the front door. I heard the car leave the driveway.

Matthias stood up and pulled me into his arms. He looked down into my eyes. "I wish I could say I knew what the future held," he paused. "For you, for me." He lowered his lips to mine. A fire lit. I wanted more, more of him. I wrapped my arms around his neck and molded our bodies together. My hands found their way up his shirt and across his chest, then down to his belt buckle. He pulled away. "No, Lindsey." Our feet hit the ground so hard I lost my balance and he had to keep me from falling. "I shouldn't even be kissing you, but it can go no further, you have to understand that." He sat me on the couch.

I didn't understand. The fire I felt was consuming, and my heart beat out of control at his touch. What was there to understand? I wanted him and I thought he wanted me, too.

"It is bad enough that I am kissing another man's wife, but I cannot and will not do anything more to ruin you." Another man's wife? Was there someone else? I was confused. "What do you mean, 'another man's wife'?"

"I have no idea who you will marry, but I'm pretty sure it's not me, and that makes you another man's wife."

That really made no sense to me. I wasn't married and had no plans of becoming so. Ruin me? What was there to ruin? So I was a virgin, but wasn't it up to me who I gave it to? Did he think I was waiting until I got married? What century was he from? Oh yeah, not mine. "You know this is the twenty-first century. Chivalry is out." I placed my hand on his thigh and slid it up. He caught my hand.

"It's not chivalry, it's a command. I am part angel, remember?"

I hadn't thought of that, but I hadn't believed in God since Mom got sick. Why should I believe now? Anger flared over Mom's death. The memory of the bright angel flashed through my head. I looked at Matthias standing in front of me. I was so confused as to what was going on.

"Just listen. I know you don't understand, but just take my word for it. I will not go there, okay?" He still had my hand. He gently pulled me back up to stand in front of him. "Okay?" he asked again.

I took a deep breath. "You're right. I don't understand." His eyes were like shiny black pearls. How could he be an angel and kiss me the way he did?

"Maybe I should just go?" He pulled away.

"No!" I didn't want him to go. "I promise to behave. How about we go do something?" That seemed to appease him for the moment.

"What about Beth? I thought you were going to the movies this weekend with her."

I had forgotten about the movies and Beth. I really didn't want to go now. Not without ... "You want to go with us?"

He smiled. "Who doesn't like Brad Pitt?" I grabbed the phone and called Beth. There was a matinee at 11:30, and we would meet her there.

Chapter 11

Normalcy

Todd and Kayla came with Beth. I was always glad to see the purple around them when they were together. At least one couple I knew was going to make it. Now, Beth was a different story altogether. She was always asking me to watch her closely when she walked by guys. Maybe I could find her "Mister Right" for her by watching her color. Todd and Kayla sat in the back row while the rest of us sat in the middle. Beth sat on one side of Matthias and I sat on the other. The movie was good, I guess, but seemed a little long.

"How about lunch?" Matthias suggested. We decided on Momma Mia's Pizzeria. It wasn't far. Matthias insisted on buying everyone's lunch. I was interested in seeing what excuse he would use to not eat, but to my surprise, he didn't make one. He ate and drank like everyone else. I touched our arms together ever so nonchalantly. I hoped he would hear me.

I thought you didn't eat. He glanced up at me as he picked up a piece of pizza to take bite.

I said I had no desire to, not that I couldn't. It really has no effect one way or the other. Blend in, remember? I looked at him. He and Todd seemed to be trying to see who could out eat each other.

"I am going to explode if I eat anymore." Matthias let Todd win. Beth and Kayla had been talking about heading to the mall, some big sale at American Eagle. So we all went. Todd and Matthias chatted about ball teams and who was going to win the championship this year as we walked up the mall to the store. I really hated the mall. I wasn't a born shopper like Beth or Kayla. They were both in seventh heaven as soon as we hit the store. I struggled just looking at the clothes. And there were a ton of them. I was sure they would have to go through all of them.

Matthias came up behind me and held out a shirt. "What do you think?" I laid my hand on his arm. *"I think I hate shopping."*

He smiled. *"Just blend in, and you'll survive."* This talking without talking could be quite handy.

I looked up at the shirt he was still holding in front of him. "Great, you'll look like one of those posters at Abercrombie if you wear that."

He put on a big grin. "So you like those posters?"

I took the shirt from his hand and held it up to his chest. "Well, it would be awfully hard to keep my hands off you if you have this on." He took it from me and put it back on the shelf. I laughed.

He turned and smiled. "So when did I need a shirt for that?" I heard Beth and Kayla giggle from behind me. I turned to find them both giving me that astounded but you-go-girl look. I turned back around, but he had taken off. I would have to get him later for that.

Before long, Beth and Kayla had an armful of clothes to try on. They had me piled down too, so we headed to the dressing rooms. The guys flopped down on the couches outside and waited for the show to begin. We each took turns parading in front of them to get a thumbs up or down. Kayla, of course, looked good in anything, so she got thumbs up every time. Beth got three ups and one down. Me, I got two up and two down. I fussed about not really liking any of the outfits, but of course it really wasn't a matter of liking them at all. It was a matter of not having the money for them. Beth and Kayla were determined that I had to have them. A treat-yourself-right gift. So when we left, I held a bag with two outfits in them. Matthias had insisted he buy them for me, so I insisted he buy the shirt he had put back. He didn't like the idea, but it was the only way I would let him buy my stuff, so he caved.

We went to two more clothing stores and three shoe stores. I had five new outfits and a pair of shoes and Matthias had three new shirts and three pairs of jeans by the time we took a breather at the food court. Todd and Kayla had ice cream, Beth had a latte, and Mathias and I had cookies. Well, I had cookies. He didn't have anything but a Coke. Which he didn't drink, so when mine ran dry, I switched them. By the time we left, it was getting late. Altogether it had been a decent day, I must admit. Not one of my favorites, but it was a bit of normalcy, which I really needed right now. I dropped the clothes bags on the floor and flopped down on the couch. I grabbed Matthias' hand and pulled him down beside me. He put his arm around me. Man, I was tired.

It was dark. I was running though a large meadow. I could hear an awful sound coming from behind me. Not really close, but it was gaining. The sound was getting closer every second. I glanced over my shoulder. I could see a red glow coming from the edge of the meadow as I ran. I was running as hard as I could, heading for the other edge. The noise was getting extremely loud now. Whatever it was, it was about to catch me. I wasn't going to make it. I stopped and turned to face it. A flash of silver came between me and the red glow. It reached for the silver. No! I screamed. The creature was holding the man in silver by his throat. His silver was flickering and turning red when another sliver glow came out from somewhere behind me and attacked the creature. *"Lindsey, let me help you."*

"Daniel?"

"I'm here, Lindsey. Just sleep."

I opened my eyes. His hand was touching my face. He did look a lot like Matthias. *"I am sorry I mistook you for Matthias."*

"Go back to sleep, Lindsey. No more bad dreams tonight." My eyes closed. Warm and sunny dreams followed.

My alarm was going off, and I opened my eyes. No, that wasn't my alarm, it was my phone. I reached for it, but it quit before I could answer. I flicked it open to see who called. No missed calls. I thought of Matthias, probably his subtle way of waking me. I needed a shower before school. Crap! I had four papers due today and had only worked on one. I hopped up and headed to the shower. Maybe I could throw something down before school. I really didn't have a prayer, but when had that ever stopped me?

A prayer, I thought. Matthias was an angel. There had to be more to that God thing. There had to be if he was an angel. Come on, Lindsey, my mind kicked in, you have no time for this now. I showered in record time and went back to my room to get dressed. I stopped when I got to the end of my bed. There lay all four papers that I had due today, neatly stacked. All the rough drafts were even there, written in my writing and everything. I smiled; he didn't miss a thing. One of the outfits he had bought me yesterday also lay beside them, all clean and ready to wear. I guess he liked this one. I laughed. He better be wearing his American Eagle shirt. I dressed and gathered up the papers. My alarm clock went off as I was heading out of my room. I shut it off and went toward the kitchen.

Dad wasn't up yet. He had worked the late shift, so it would be a few hours before he stirred. My nose caught a whiff of something wonderful as I entered the kitchen. Two big hot blueberry muffins sat on a plate on the table beside a glass of milk. "Okay." I turned to look around the kitchen. He appeared in the chair across from the muffins.

"Good morning."

I sat down in the chair and started eating. "Sorry I fell asleep on you last night."

"That's okay, you were worn out. Did you sleep well?"

"Once your brother showed up, I did."

"Same dream?" he asked.

"Yeah." I smiled. "You'll be glad to know I didn't assault your brother last night." He chuckled. "You two sure look a lot alike when it's dark. I think he was relieved when I called him by his own name instead of yours."

"Did you talk to him?"

"No, not really. Well, I did tell him I was sorry for thinking he was you. He didn't say much, though. He just kept telling me to go back to sleep."

Beth honked out in the drive. "I'll see you at school," he said and was gone, along with the plate and glass.

I grabbed my stuff and headed for Beth's car. Beth had a huge grin on her face when I got in. "Well, I want to know all about it." I knew this was coming, but I just didn't know what to tell her.

I looked at her and smiled. "Well, he is a great guy. I really like him a lot."

She rolled her eyes at me. "Who do you think you're kidding? I was with you all day yesterday. I saw how you two looked and acted toward each other." We were still sitting in front of the house.

"Beth, we may want to go to school." She pushed the gear shift up to park.

"Nope. I don't care if we are late. Talk to me."

"Well, he's a great kisser."

She smiled. "And?"

I looked at her. "And what?"

"How about the rest of him?"

I turned red. "I wouldn't know."

She looked at me. "Sure. I heard him say you couldn't keep your hands off him, so spill it."

I shook my head. "He said that because you and Kayla were listening, but there is really nothing to spill. All we did was kiss. I promise you." She looked disappointed. She put the car in drive and took off. "Good grief, Beth. You thought we did more?"

She smiled as we pulled into the parking lot. "Well I would have." I wasn't going to tell her I tried and he turned me down. "So are you dating now?"

Dating. I really hadn't thought of that. I really didn't know. "I'm not sure. We haven't really talked about it, and you know I am new to this whole boyfriend concept." We both laughed as we got out.

"Yeah, but it's about time." She pointed toward the school doors. There he stood, in his AE shirt. I hadn't noticed if he had it on at the house earlier, but I noticed now. He really could put any of those posters to shame.

"Hey, Beth," he said as we approached.

"You know, she was right about the shirt. It does make you look like one of those guys in the posters, especially with your hair down."

He grinned. "Thanks." He took my books and walked me to my first class. "See you in an hour." I watched him walk back down the hall.

"Come on." Beth pulled me into the room. Everyone seemed to be staring at me.

"I told you that you looked good in that outfit," Kayla said as I sat down. Her desk was behind mine. Great, I thought. Kayla must have told everyone in school about us. And if Beth thought we were doing it, then so did Kayla and now everyone else, too. Matthias wouldn't like that. Well, it was his fault. He was the one that made the comment about me not keeping my hands off him. I was so glad when the bell finally rang for second period. I walked to Mrs. Hawthorne's class. I felt like I had a sign or something pinned to me. People were staring. Matthias was already sitting at his desk behind mine. I dropped my books on the desk and glared at him. "I shouldn't have made the remark in the store, should I?"

"Ya think?" I sat down.

"So what's the total damage?"

I had to laugh. "Well, the whole school thinks we're sleeping together." I wasn't being too quiet.

"But we're not."

"Well, I know that, but thanks to your comment, everyone thinks we are." There, maybe that was loud enough to put a stop to some of the rampant rumors.

The bell rang and class got started. We handed in our report. It was actually just over twenty pages. Matthias explained that he just couldn't get all his comments in on twenty; I had taken up too many pages.

"Everyone else had an oral test, but I am going to give you an essay test, so head back down to the study hall and hand these in to Mrs. Jones at the end of the hour," Mrs. Hawthorne told us. So once again we headed for the library. Matthias was right behind me.

"I will be so glad when school is out," I said as I sat my books down on the desk. I sat down and started writing. I looked up to find Matthias just staring at me. I tried to write, but it was hard with him staring. "Please stop. I need to concentrate." He turned and looked out the window. I could see his test was already done. I moved my leg over and touched his.

"I want to ask you something."

"Sure, what is it?" Neither one of us said a word out loud.

"How is it that if you're this angel and you're supposed to answer to God, you are also helping me cheat?"

He looked up at me. *"What are you talking about?"*

"You did all my reports for me. Isn't that cheating?"

He smiled. *"No. I didn't do them. You did them this morning when you thought about what you would have put in them. I was just the pencil you used."*

"What?"

Matthias smiled at me. *"Don't you think God knows what your ability is? He is the one who made you."*

I moved my leg and looked at my paper. He smiled and turned back toward the window. More things I just didn't understand. When the bell rang, we handed in our tests and headed to lunch. I stopped before going through the doors. I really didn't want to go and have everyone staring at us.

"Come on." Matthias pulled on my arm. I sat down at the table. "You want anything?" he asked.

"No, thanks. I had a big breakfast." He sat down beside me.

Todd and Kayla came in. "Hey man," Todd said. "The first baseball game of the season is Tuesday night. Everybody's coming over to watch the game. You should come."

Mike and Kyle walked by, and most people noticed their all-black attire. I just noticed their colors of blue. "Your house, Tuesday night, right?"

Todd turned. "Yep, you bring chips." He turned back to Matthias. "So, you going to come?"

"I might. What do I need to bring if I do?"

"A case of drinks." Todd turned, sat down, and started talking to Kayla. Michelle came over and whispered in Kayla's ear. I smiled. Michelle had been in my last class so I knew she was telling all she had heard to Kayla. Michelle finally stood up.

"Hey Lindsey, Dad wanted to know when he could expect you back at work?"

"Oh, tell him I am sorry. I meant to call him this weekend, but I got a little overwhelmed with all the work I have to make up. I can work Tuesday and Thursday this week and then come back on full schedule next week, if that's okay?"

She smiled. "I will be glad when you're back. I am the one that's been filling in and I don't like all the classes you teach."

I looked at her. "Sorry, Chelle."

She smiled at me. "It's really not all that bad. I am just tired of Dad telling me how great an asset you are to the gym." She said it in her best "dad" voice. Everybody laughed.

"So what kind of classes do you teach?" Matthias asked.

"I teach four aerobics classes and two yoga classes."

"Wow," he said. "That explains all the health food in your kitchen." He played dumb really well. With Matthias around, I hadn't even thought about work. But with all the bills now coming in, I sure needed to get back to it.

Lunch ended and the next two classes flew by because of tests I had to take in them. By fourth period, most of the staring had stopped, thank goodness. What I was really looking forward to today was getting back to gym class, but leave it to Mr. Holland not to let me do a lot. I guess anything was better than nothing. After class I met Beth at her car.

"I think I am going to walk home," I told her. Matthias was standing behind me.

She smiled. "Okay." She leaned over and whispered, "Don't do anything I wouldn't."

I laughed and shook my head. She got in her car and drove off. Next week I would get my keys back and would be able to drive if I wanted to, but I would most likely just keep walking. Matthias and I headed down the sidewalk.

"You look tired," Matthias told me.

"I am. Today was my first day back in gym, but I don't know why I am so tired. Mr. Holland didn't let me do much of anything."

Matthias laughed. "It's probably good he didn't. You better work your way back up to everything you were doing." He was right. I better keep it light for a little while and work my way back up. I just hoped I could make it through my classes tomorrow night at the gym.

"I better call Mr. Ziggler and ask if I can only do one class tomorrow night instead of two. Poor Michelle. She is not going to like that."

We walked up on the porch and Matthias opened the door for me. I dropped my books on the table. "You need to rest and you need Daniel for that, so I am going to split. I'll see you later, okay?"

"I'm fine," I told him.

He looked at me. "You can't fool me. Go take a nap. I'll come by later."

I caved. "Alright." I really was beat. I went to my room and crashed on the bed. I started to drift off. Something warm was on my face. I opened my eyes and smiled at Daniel. He smiled back as I drifted back off.

Chapter 12

God

When I woke, Daniel still hovered above me. He smiled and disappeared. It was late; it had already gotten dark outside. Dad would be home anytime. I headed for the kitchen. I needed to get supper at least started before he got home.

"Finally, you're awake." Matthias stood behind me. I jumped when he spoke. "Sorry, didn't mean to startle you."

I turned around to face him. "I need to get supper going, and no, there is no cheating."

He smiled as I turned back around and started pulling stuff out of the fridge. "Can I help then?"

"Go light the grill, then you can cut up this eggplant."

Matthias went right to work on the eggplant. "Grill's lit," he said. I looked up at him. "Sorry," he laughed.

"Hey, can I ask you something?"

"Sure."

"I've been thinking. If you're an angel, then all that God stuff you hear about is true?"

He looked up at me. "If you mean that He created the universe and sent His son to die and save us, if you mean all that stuff, then yeah, it's true." He smiled at me then looked toward the door, set down the knife, kissed me on the forehead, then vanished.

"Something smells good," Dad said as he came through the door.

Supper was good! "Lindz?" Dad asked as we washed the dishes.

"Yeah, Dad?"

"How have you been feeling?"

I turned and smiled at him. "I'm fine, Dad. If I start feeling bad, you'll be the first to know."

He smiled back. "I feel like I haven't seen you in weeks."

"I know. You've been working a lot and I have had a ton of schoolwork. Maybe things will get back to normal soon and we can head to the mountains for a weekend."

"I agree," he said. "You feel like a run with the old man?"

"Sounds great." I headed for my room to change. I was charged from my nap and ready to go. I changed into sweats and running shoes and headed back toward the living room. Dad was already waiting by the door when I got to end of the hall. It had been at least a month since we had gotten to go running together. I had missed it. I liked being out in nature, but I loved the city at night. Most of the traffic was gone and the city was cool and calm. Most people had already settled in for the night. Well, there was always someone out in the city, but that was okay. The air was cool and felt good. I caught a glimmer of silver as we passed by an alley. I wondered if it was Matthias or Daniel. We used to run for a least an hour, but neither of us had been doing anything lately, so we decided thirty minutes would be good.

"Thanks, Dad. I have missed our late-night runs."

"Me too, Lindz. Me too."

I headed for the shower. The water was hot and felt good. I had a feeling I would be sore tomorrow. I put my pj's on and headed to bed. I lay back on my bed, closed my eyes, and waited. So the God thing was real. So why did Mom die? She had believed in him. Anger flared. Why had he let her die? A thought crossed my mind. It was something Mom had told me before she died. "God has a plan for you, Lindsey." Was she talking about now, about the cancer? How could giving me cancer be a plan unless it was to kill me? I wanted answers! I hadn't prayed since Mom died. "Okay, God, I need to know. Why did Mom die? Why did you give me cancer?" Matthias entered my mind. "Why have you sent Matthias and Daniel? Why is this demon attacking me?" I lay there waiting for answers. How did God answer prayers? I really wasn't sure. I felt a warm hand on my face. I opened my eyes. Daniel was there.

"It will all be fine, you'll see. Don't worry, Lindsey. He knows what He's doing." He smiled. I closed my eyes again. That wasn't the answer I wanted, but suddenly I felt calm and tired.

I woke early. My dreams were fine, but I just couldn't seem to lie there anymore.

Daniel smiled when I opened my eyes. *"You're awake early."*

"Big day today. I go back to work. Hey, can I ask you something?"

"Sure." Daniel removed his hand from my face.

"Where do you go in the daytime?"

He chuckled. "Don't worry. I'm always close. You're never out of my sight."

"Why don't you talk to Matthias?"

Daniel got a stressed look on his face. "I will when I need to, but now is not the time." He vanished then.

I got out of the bed and watched the sunrise from my window. I had two classes tonight, one aerobics, and one yoga. I thought I would call Mr. Ziggler and tell him I couldn't do both. Then I decided if I just kept the yoga to mainly all stretching and slowly worked back into the full strength training of it then I could keep the class. Now what to wear? I opened my closet and looked at my clothes. I pulled out a new pair of jeans and a blue button-down fitted shirt that I had gotten at the mall with Matthias. I got dressed and then sat down on the bed to tie my shoes.

"Did you have a good night with your dad?" Matthias was now standing at my door.

"One of these days you're going to pop in and I won't be dressed."

He smiled. "No, I always make sure you're dressed."

"And how do you do that?"

He thought for a minute. "Well ... not real sure, but I always know."

I finished tying my shoes, gathered up my books, and put them in my bag. "Matthias?" I sat back down on the bed.

"Yeah?" He walked over, sat down beside me, and touched my arm. *"Your dad is waking up."* He was now talking to me in my head.

"How do you know what you're supposed to do? I mean do you talk to God or ... well, how does it work?"

He smiled at me. *"For the most part, Daniel's the one that gets the word of what and where we are supposed to go and do. I just heal or protect, and occasionally Daniel helps."*

"So Daniel's not a healer?"

"Not usually. That's why I was worried when I couldn't find him. He plans, I heal or protect. And on occasion, we protect together, but we have never done separate things."

I heard the bathroom door shut. *"So, what does he do when you're healing?"*

"Restores houses. He actually does it. It's not just a cover for him."

I got up and grabbed my purse and bag. Then I laid my arm back on his. *"How about some breakfast?"*

"What do you want? I'll meet you at the front door with it."

I smiled and kissed him. *"How about some of those big muffins and a cappuccino?"*

"Is that what your dad will want, too?"

"He will want black coffee instead of a cappuccino, but the muffins will be fine with him." He got up, kissed me on the forehead, and vanished. I almost collided with Dad as he came out of the bathroom.

"Morning, Dad."

"Morning, sweetie." Dad followed me to the kitchen. Matthias knocked on the door as Dad walked by it. "Who in the world?" Dad said as he turned to open the door.

"Morning, sir," I heard Matthias say. "How about a muffin and some coffee?"

"Love some," Dad said as he stepped aside for Matthias to enter. I smiled as Matthias laid a bag of muffins on the table and three cups.

"Black," he said and handed one to Dad. "French vanilla cappuccino." He handed me one.

"And what is yours?" I asked.

"They had a cinnamon swirl cappuccino I thought I would try." He opened the bag. "We have blueberry, banana nut, and an apple cinnamon."

"I'll have a banana nut," Dad said.

"Here you are." He handed Dad a muffin.

"Awful nice of you to bring breakfast by, Matthias."

Matthias smiled at Dad. "I was hoping Lindsey would let me walk her to school." Dad laughed and looked at me.

"Well, I guess since you brought breakfast, I can't refuse," I told him as I looked at Dad.

"You better call Beth," Dad told me, so I got my phone out and sent her a text. Dad and Matthias sat down at the table and ate. "Lindz says you just moved here?" Dad asked Matthias.

"Yes, sir. My brother restores houses. He is working on the Ashford house over on Oak."

"The big orange brick one?" Dad asked.

"Yep, that's the one. It is in pretty bad shape, but Daniel will have it fixed in no time."

"I hear that place was used in the Underground Railroad."

Matthias smiled. "It was. There are secret tunnels and rooms all through it. Would you like to see it sometime?"

Dad lit up. "I would love to. Do you think your brother will mind?"

"Oh, no. I am sure he won't, but I'll ask, just to make sure." Dad smiled up at me.

"We need to go, Dad."

Dad looked at his watch and then finished his muffin and grabbed his coffee. "Thanks for breakfast, Matthias."

"Anytime, sir." Matthias grabbed my book bag off the floor and walked to the door.

"See you later, Dad."

"Have a good day, Lindz." I gave Dad a quick hug and Matthias and I left. Dad was right behind us and pulled out of the driveway as we turned the corner.

"What?" Matthias asked.

"How is Daniel working on the house and watching me at the same time, or is that a silly question?"

Matthias laughed. "No, it's not silly. Since he has been with you at night, I have been working on the house for him. I must admit I cheat a lot on the working part. I am not good with tools like Daniel is." So Daniel actually did his work. It had to be great to work and never get tired.

"It must be nice to never get tired and have to sleep."

Matthias looked at me. "Not really. How would you like for the day to never end?" I had not thought of it like that. "Time really has no meaning. As for not being tired, I think I do get tired, just not physically. Don't get me wrong, I am thankful for not being a demon and I love helping people, but it just never ends."

I felt sorry for Matthias and Daniel. How hard would it be to never start a new day. I took Matthias' hand in mine as we walked toward the school. "Do you ever feel like quitting, or can you?"

He stopped walking and looked at me. "I don't really know. I mean I wouldn't want to be doing anything else, so why would I want to quit?" He smiled at me. "Well, I can think of only one reason I would want to quit, and until now, it was never an issue." He was talking about me. I smiled as we walked on toward school. What was I doing? I was tempting an angel. Would I be cursed and damned to hell?

Matthias answered my thought. "You're not, Lindsey. Don't even think like that." He held the door as we entered the school. I sat in first period, but all I could think about was Matthias. Second period, Mrs. Hawthorne had us watch a movie, but my mind was still wandering some. Matthias touched my leg with his foot.

"I don't have to be reading your mind to see the worry on your face."

"If only I could be so calm about the whole situation."

"You know what I do when something bothers me? I take it right to the Maker himself."

Talking to God. I had said a prayer before, but I guess I hadn't really given a lot a thought about talking to God. But I guess if they were angels, they talked to him all the time. Matthias snickered from behind me. Okay, so I was new to this God thing.

Chapter 13

Graduation

The sun was bright when I woke. Graduation day was finally here. The last few weeks of school had finally gone by and things were mainly back to normal, with a few exceptions. Matthias had become a regular at the house. Dad loved it when he cooked breakfast on Sunday mornings. Matthias checked me to see if my cancer or not cancer was the same every few days. We had also had several discussions on angels, demons, and God. We had even gone to church one Sunday. Dad hadn't gone with us, but I think with a little nudge I might be able to get him to go. To my surprise, the day we did go I came home with a real sense of peace. Daniel appeared every night, so I slept with not a single nightmare. Life seemed to be good, at least for the moment, and tonight we graduated. This time tomorrow I would be camping in the park. Dad had surprised me one Sunday morning by asking Matthias to go with us. What could be better than hiking and camping with the guys I loved?

The smell of breakfast cooking made my stomach growl. I hopped out of bed and headed for the kitchen. Dad had taken the day off for graduation and then the weekend for camping. I was so glad to see him glowing bright blue these days. He was sitting at the table, and of course, Matthias was in front of the stove.

"Good morning, Daddy." I kissed him on the cheek then went and put my arms around Matthias.

"You're going to make me burn this." He turned and gave me a quick kiss on the head and turned back. I retreated to the chair across from Dad.

"Man, that smells great. What is it?"

"Not sure. I saw it on the Food Network, but I didn't catch the name." Playing dumb again. I knew he didn't miss anything. "Your dad offered to be the guinea pig for me."

I looked at Dad who was now smiling. "I told him I would suffer through." We both giggled.

"Well, it's done, I think." He dropped two helpings on plates and set them in front of us. It smelled heavenly. I took a bite and then wrinkled my nose. I put my hand up and pushed Dad's fork away from his mouth.

"Dad, don't eat it." He looked shocked. "I think you better give it to me. He can make you something else." It was hard keeping my face steady. Dad's eyes were big. I glanced over at Matthias. The look of terror was on his face. He was really wondering if he had made something that tasted bad. I rolled with laughter. "You should have seen your faces! It was priceless." Matthias gave me a little punch. Dad just rolled his eyes.

"You got us." He took a big bite. "Fabulous, Matthias, just fabulous."

After breakfast was cleaned up, we headed to school for yet another graduation practice. How many times did they think it took you to learn to march up the aisle, across the stage, and out? Evidently we couldn't practice enough for Ms. Julie. She was so stressed about it all that she was turning slightly orange. Todd, Kayla, and Beth met us at Momma Mia's for lunch after practice. Todd's parents were throwing a big graduation party for the whole class at the country club right after graduation. Todd had hired a band and was telling Matthias about them. None of us had heard of them, but according to Todd they were up and coming.

"I am heading to check out the dorm rooms at Harvard this weekend," Beth was telling Kayla. "Mom is insistent that if I want a good room, I better go stake claim to it."

"I figured your parents would get you an apartment." Of course Kayla had an apartment already waiting at the University of Kentucky. She thought everyone should have their own. "Of course they would have gotten me one," Beth told her, "but the dorm is coed and I hear the guys are hot." Leave it to Beth to find a guy angle. "You have to come visit me during the year, Lindz."

"Me too," piped in Kayla. Both of them knew I couldn't afford college. Dad and I barely made it month to month now that all the medical bills had started coming in, but they didn't know that. Really, I hadn't given college much thought lately anyway. I would really just like to travel. See the U.S. and maybe an overseas place or two. I would have to do some saving, but I liked that a whole lot better than even thinking about going to school again. We spent most of the afternoon there just talking.

After that, we all headed home to get ready. Matthias' stuff was at the house. Matthias had given Dad a story about Daniel being called back to France, about there being some kind of problem with the house he had just finished so that Dad wouldn't be freaked out when Daniel didn't show. Dad met us at the front door.

"Hey guys, look who made it back in time." Daniel was sitting on the couch all sliver and sparkling. He stood up. I launched myself into his arms.

"I am glad you got to come."

He smiled. "Me too."

"Glad you made it back, bro," Matthias said from behind me. I slid out of Daniel's arms just in time not to get squished. "It's not every day your little brother graduates from high school."

I wrapped an arm around each of theirs. *"I love you guys."* They both smiled down at me. "You two better get dressed," Daniel said.

I started to let go. *"I love you, too."* Matthias squeezed my arm then let me go. I headed for my room. Matthias headed to the bathroom. I fell on my bed. He loved me. I was screaming it in my head over and over. Suddenly, I was aware I wasn't alone. I bolted up and into his arms. The flames lit and he was holding me and kissing me with one arm and holding us away from the ceiling with the other. *"Put us down. We need to finish getting ready."* I backed the flames down until we were on the floor. He gave me another quick kiss and disappeared.

I picked up my dress from the bed. It was going to be a great night. I changed and looked in the mirror. I pulled my hair up and put a few traces of makeup on. I looked in the mirror once more. I usually didn't like pink, but this dress was great. It came to just below my knees and was almost strapless; it had a string going around my neck which I could have tucked in to make it strapless, but I didn't. They were all waiting on me when I got back to the living room.

"You look beautiful, babe." Dad gave me a quick kiss.

"I agree," Mathias said. Daniel gave me once over then thumbs up, with a big smile.

Dad dropped us off at the back door then he and Daniel went around to the front.

"Find your places." Ms. Julie had a bullhorn and was trying to get everyone ready to march in. She was so stressed she was a bright orange. I was up front in the Bs. Matthias was more toward the middle. I stood in line silently; I had been waiting for this day so long. I was ready not to have to get up and go to school. I really didn't care what the future held. As long as there was Matthias and no school, I would be happy. The music started and the line moved. Finally, we all made it out to our chairs. Todd was valedictorian and gave a great speech about future plans and high school friends. He added a plug for the party at the end. Everyone seemed to be excited about it, so I had no doubt everyone would be there. We all stood as Ms. Julie came to the microphone. As she read each name, the line moved. "Lindsey Nicole Black." I headed up to the podium and across the stage to get my diploma. I could hear Dad and Daniel giving some big cheers as I took my diploma with one hand and Mr. Dillingham's hand with the other. I followed the line back around to my spot. Soon I heard Matthias' name. "Matthias Matthew Johns." I didn't know his middle name was Matthew. I sort of giggled. All three of his names were first names. Matthew was also Dad's first name. The line moved slowly, but finally they called Chelle. "Michelle Renee Ziggler." She was the last one in line. A few more words from Principal Dillingham and we would be free. I threw my hat with glee high into the air when the time came.

"We finally made it!" Beth was the first to find me through the crowd. I gave her a big hug. "I am going to miss you so much when I move." Beth got close and whispered in my ear, "How am I going to know if I meet Mr. Right?" We both laughed. "You and Matthias coming out to the club?"

I smiled. "Of course, wouldn't miss it." She gave me a quick hug and headed for Kayla. I saw Matthias over at the side trying to move, but I think every girl in school was lined up to give him a congratulatory hug. I couldn't help but laugh. He was being very polite and hugging each one, but you could see the silent pleading look on his face. I smiled and started his way.

"You look great, Lindsey." Todd tackled me from behind. I turned to face him.

"Thanks, you clean up pretty good, too. Great speech."

"Thanks. You and Matthias are coming to the party aren't you?"

"Of course."

"See you there." He gave me a quick kiss on the cheek. "You really do look nice." I smiled at him, and he grinned and took off.

It took me awhile, but I finally made my way through the sea of blues and pinks to where Matthias was stuck. "You ready?" He was being hugged by a yet another girl who dropped the hug really quick when I showed up at his arm.

"Yep, let's find Daniel and your dad and get out of here." It wasn't going to be hard to find Daniel with his silver glow. We made our way through the crowd to the front doors. Dad and Daniel were outside already. Dad gave me a big hug, then gave Matthias one, too.

"Congratulations, you two."

"Thanks, Dad."

Daniel followed suit with the big hugs. "What time does Todd's party start?" he asked.

"At nine, but it won't get cranked up until ten I'm sure." I knew Daniel and Matthias wanted to do some talking. "Why don't you two do some catching up and I'll meet you at the party, say around 10:30?"

Matthias gave me a big smile. "That would be great."

"Come on. I will drop y'all off," Dad said.

"That's okay. It is a nice night and you get a lot of talking done while you're walking. But thanks," Daniel told Dad.

"All right," Dad said. "I offered."

Matthias gave me a quick hug and kiss on the forehead. "See you in a couple of hours."

I put my arm through Dad's and we headed for the car. "Man, they look a lot alike."

I laughed. "I think it would be really easy to get them confused in the dark," I said. Of course, I had experience in that area, so I knew that for a fact.

"So, what do you want to do before the party?"

I smiled up at him. "I would really like to go for a run." Dad smiled. "I was hoping you might say that." We got in the car and headed for home. I loved running with Dad. It was sort of a special dad/daughter thing.

We were changed and out on the street in ten minutes. The air was cool and felt wonderful. "What are you thinking about doing now that you have officially graduated?" Dad asked.

"I am not really sure. Been thinking about it quite a bit though." We turned a corner and headed up another street.

"What's Matthias thinking about doing?" That's what he really wanted to know; did we have plans.

"I don't know. Maybe he will take your advice and find a good culinary school." Another blocked passed. "I figure it will really have to do with Daniel. I don't think he will up and leave his brother."

"They seem really close."

"They are. I guess when they lost their parents they survived by relying on each other."

We made two laps around the park and headed on uptown to the business district. There was hardly anyone there this time of night, so you didn't have to dodge anyone much.

"You remember the list I made on the way to Kentucky?"

"Yeah."

"Well, I was still thinking about doing some of those things. Maybe work awhile and then travel awhile, then work awhile, then off. Not real sure though."

"Well, at least you sort of have a plan. It's not too bad, either. Gives you a goal to work toward." I knew he would understand my wanting to do the things on my list. He was the best!

"You know what I am really looking forward to?" He glanced over at me. "Spending the weekend with you."

"And Matthias," he added.

"You invited him, but yeah, him too. Thanks for inviting him."

"I thought you might like it if he went. You two seem to be pretty close." Oh great. He is going to give me a talk on boys. I thought for a second.

"Yeah, I guess we are, but I am not sure where it's heading yet, but I do love him being around." I hoped that would keep the talk to a bare minimum.

"Well, just don't go jumping into things you shouldn't. You know what I mean. Use some common sense and restraint."

I almost laughed. "You don't have to worry, Dad. He is really old fashioned when it comes to moving along baselines." I heard Dad breathe a sigh of relief. We had made it through the business district and were now heading back toward the park.

"Are you coming to the party, Lindsey?" Michelle was hanging out a car window as it passed.

"I'll be there in a little while," I hollered back at her.

"Okay, see you then. Hi, Mr. Black." She gave Dad a quick wave. Dad waved back.

"I bet the Parkers went all out on this party," Dad said.

"I know they did. I have heard Todd talking about it for weeks now."

I headed straight to the shower when we got back. I got dressed and grabbed my keys as I headed for the door.

"I know you won't, but don't do anything stupid," Dad said as I passed him.

I laughed. "You wouldn't be a good parent if you didn't tell me that, Dad. And don't worry. I won't." The door closed behind me. It would only take about ten minutes to get to the party. I had to admit I was looking forward to it.

The parking lot was packed. I knew everyone would come. Todd was great at catering to everyone, so I was sure he had stuff set up for everybody. I finally found a place to park and headed in. I could hear the band before I got to the front doors. The convention hall was off of the main entrance, and the band was really getting the party on. I glanced in the doors. It was a mosh pit. So cool. All the colors made it that much cooler. Too bad no one else could see them. I could hear yelling from down the hall. I wandered over to see what else was going on. A huge projection screen was set up and had a baseball game showing on it. Down further, another room was full of kids playing video games. I think I counted five systems hooked together. Leave it to Todd; it was going to be the party of the century.

"Hey, I was wondering when you would show." It was Beth. "I heard Cullen and Christy decided to break up for college." She was grinning from ear to ear. She had always had a thing for Cullen.

"Don't do anything stupid."

"I would never," she grinned, and we headed back down to the pit. "Look, there he is. He is so gorgeous." There were bodies moving in rhythm everywhere. "Come on." She pulled me toward the mass of bodies. "I better lay claim to him before someone else does." Beth was such a player.

The music was great. Todd was right about the band. They were definitely up and coming.

"Hey, glad you made it." It was Kayla. She and Todd were coming out of the mass. "Dance with her for awhile. I am going for a drink." Kayla pushed Todd on me. He smiled and grabbed my hand and pulled me back in the mass of moving bodies. I wasn't a dancer, but who couldn't jump up and down? It was great. Todd was having a blast. He kept rubbing up and down against me, but so were the other three people on my sides.

"Hey, man, can I cut in?" It was Matthias.

"Sure, come on." Todd just turned to the person beside him and kept jumping. Matthias pulled our bodies together and we moved in unison. He had on jeans and his white shirt from graduation, no tie. Both sleeves were rolled up and his shirt was about halfway unbuttoned. He was so hot looking. Our bodies were molded together. I could feel the flames wanting to lift us off the floor. He must have felt the same; his eyes were so intense and they swirled with heat.

He took my hand and pulled me through the crowd, out the side door across the golf course to a small wooded area. As soon as we were out of sight from all sides, he pulled me into his arms and his lips crushed down on mine. He caught a limb and held us there so we didn't fly out over the tops of the trees. His lips slid down my neck. I exploded inside. His bare chest felt so good against me. I kissed across it and back up to his lips. *"Lindsey."* I loved the way our bodies felt against each other, skin against skin. "Lindsey!" he yelled this time. Skin against skin! Flame went out. I dropped. He caught me before I could hit the ground. I looked down. His white shirt was gone and he now had on a blue t-shirt. I had on different clothes, too. I looked up and saw anger in his eyes. He sat me down on my feet.

"I ..."

"Forget it. I was the one who pushed it tonight. I knew better." He took my hand and led me back out of the woods.

"I think someone might notice us wearing different clothes."

He stopped and turned to face me. "I don't know what you did with our other clothes." He had spoken slowly and steadily as if he wanted to yell at me, but was holding back. I looked up at him. Our clothes changed. "Happy?" He turned and headed back.

When we got back into the party, I saw Beth. She had evidently won her prize. Cullen had his arms around her waist and was kissing her neck. I smiled, still no purple. She smiled as she saw us come through the doors. Matthias led us back to where the band was playing. He leaned back on the wall and pulled me in front of him. He slid his arms around me and locked them in front. I leaned back against him. *"Behave yourself,"* he told me in my head.

"I'm sorry. I just lost it back there."

"Well, I guess we now know something else you can do." I didn't reply to that.

After about forty minutes, the band took a break and people scattered all though the building and out on the grounds.

"I think I am ready to leave. How about you?"

He smiled. "Come on." He took my hand and we headed for the parking lot.

"You aren't leaving are you?" I heard Todd running to catch up with us. I turned.

"Dad is taking us hiking and camping tomorrow, and I don't want to be dragging."

"Well, I guess I better not hold you up then, but I am glad you guys came." He gave me a hug and Matthias one of those manly shoulder bumps. "You guys be safe going home and have a great trip."

"The party is great, Todd. They'll be talking about it for a long time." He gave me a great big smile and headed back. He gave a quick wave as he headed in the doors. "So how is Daniel?" I asked as we got in the car.

"He's good. Not so happy with me, but he's good."

"What is he not happy about?" He turned to look at me. Oh, us. "What did he say?"

"He is quite angry that I am leading you on since my future is not here. He couldn't understand that I have these feelings that erupted in me when you were near." I smiled. He had feelings that erupted when I was near. "I know I probably wouldn't have believed it either if it weren't happening to me."

I laid my hand on his arm as he drove. "Sorry." We didn't say much the rest of the way home. He pulled in the driveway then turned to look at me.

"I don't know what is going to happen once you're healed or whatever, but you have to know I have never felt this way before. I can't ever remember even getting close to someone, ever. I don't want to hurt you, Lindsey."

I put my hand up. "Just stop right there. I know you have no clue about what the future holds for you, or even if you'll be here tomorrow. Can't we just be happy now and let the future worry about itself? If you're gone tomorrow ... well, I'll hurt, but I'll know you had to go and it was out of your hands and ..." He picked up my sentence.

"... and that I love you."

I smiled. "I love you, too." He leaned over the console and gently kissed me. "I will see you tomorrow." He smiled and then vanished. I slid over the console and got out the driver's door. The house was dark, so Dad hadn't waited up. I about half expected him to. I headed in and to the bathroom to shower again. I just couldn't even think about sleeping knowing I had had all those sweaty bodies rubbing up against me in the mosh pit. I looked at the clothes on the floor; I wondered where my others were. I couldn't believe I took our clothes off. It hadn't hit me until then that maybe I could do things like him, move things. Ohh, the easy way, I thought. I stood in the shower for ten minutes just trying to move the shampoo off the wire rack. It wasn't working. I lay on my bed thinking about what he said about Daniel. I closed my eyes. Come on, Daniel. Where are you? Thirty minutes passed, still no Daniel. He knew I would be waiting to talk to him, so he wasn't going to come until I fell asleep.

It was dark; I was running in the meadow again. I could hear the creature; it was behind me. It was gaining on me every second. I glanced over my shoulder and I could see the glow of red behind me. I wasn't going to make it. I stopped and turned to face it. A flash of silver came between us. The creature reached for the silver. No! I screamed. The creature was holding Daniel by his throat. His silver was flickering. Another sliver glow came out from somewhere behind me and attacked the creature. He now held both Daniel and Matthias by their necks. I was scared. No, I was angry. Angry that he had them. He was not going to hurt them again. I set my feet; he could not have them. *"Lindsey, come on. Let the dream go. I am here."* The scene faded, but I was still mad. It was filling my every fiber.

"Lindsey." The voice was not in my head. My eyes jerked open. Daniel was up against the ceiling.

"Daniel?" He dropped, but stopped just above me.

"You can move things!" It was a statement, not a question.

"Sorry, I didn't hurt you, did I?" He touched my face.

"No, I haven't felt pain in a hundred and seventy years. Sorry I wasn't here to keep you from having the nightmare again. I knew you would want to talk before you went to sleep and I didn't want to."

"You're right, I did. And I still do." I took a deep breath. *"You have to understand. I know that tomorrow Matthias could be gone. It's not up to him. I understand that, but can't I just love him while he is here?"*

Daniel closed his eyes for a second then opened them back. *"I am not going to tell you I understand any of this, especially you, but I know it's not up to me. I am not the one with the big picture, so I am going to leave it at that. I do know, however, that you make him happy, happier than I have ever seen him, so by all means, you guys make each other happy for as long as you can. Just remember that there will be a day coming that he has to leave, and nothing you can do will change it."*

I smiled, I thought of how happy Matthias would be to hear that Daniel had come around. A little flame lit at the thought of him. I used it to pull Daniel close enough to give a quick kiss on the cheek, and then let him go. *"Thanks,"* I said and then I closed my eyes and wandered off to sleep.

Chapter 14

A Beginning in the End

I woke to Daniel whispering in my head, his hand warm on my cheek. *"Your dad has been pacing the hall for an hour."* I opened my eyes. *"I thought he was coming in once and that I would have to leave."*

"I better get up then." He smiled and vanished. I opened my door to find Dad just outside. He tried to look as if he was just heading to the bathroom.

"You up already? I figured you would stay out late and wouldn't get up until noon."

I smiled. "Did you, now? Well, I figured you would let me sleep instead of pacing the hall this morning." He had been caught and he knew it.

"Was I that loud?"

"No, we didn't stay very long at the party. I wanted to be ready for hiking and not be dragging like a zombie."

He smiled really big. "Then what are we waiting for? Get Matthias on the phone and tell him to come on." I headed to the bathroom to wash up. "Nevermind," I heard Dad yell from the kitchen. "He's here." I got dressed, gathered up all my gear, and headed down the hall. I could smell muffins. Dad was digging into a bag that Matthias had brought with him.

"Muffin?" I dropped my stuff and walked over and put my arms around him. He smiled down at me.

"Load 'er up. Let's get on the road." Dad had a muffin in one hand and a cup of coffee in the other. He had loaded his stuff already, most likely at dawn. Matthias grabbed my stuff.

"You get the muffins and coffee." I grabbed them and followed him out. We were going to Starved Rock State Park which was only a little over an hour to the southwest, but that was okay. It was a great park and we only had two nights, so we had to make the best out of it. I let Matthias sit up front with Dad. I sat watching through my window as the city melted away into the forests. We pulled up to the park entrance and Bill was at the guard shack. We came often enough that he knew us by name.

"Matt, it's been awhile. Hey, Lindsey. I thought you had dropped off the face of the earth. It's been over three months since you were here last."

Dad smiled. "Been busy. Lindsey graduated last night and this is what she wanted for graduation."

"Good call, Lindsey." I smiled.

"Bill, this is Matthias. He is a friend of Lindsey's."

Matthias reached across and shook Bill's hand. "Nice to meet you, sir."

"So how long you guys staying?" It was Bill's job to know who was in the park and how long they were staying.

"Tonight and tomorrow night."

"Alright then, I'll sign you in. You guys have a great time. Congrats, Lindsey."

"Thanks."

We drove past the main buildings and past the campgrounds to the campers' parking area. There were maybe ten cars there. Great! It wasn't going to be crowded. We got our gear out. My backpack wasn't very heavy. Dad always carried the most weight, but this time he and Matthias split it. Dad and I knew already where we would pitch our tent for the night. It was by a stream about fifteen miles in, but it was a great spot. We hiked all morning, took a break about noon to snack a little, and then headed back out. The weather was perfect, warm and mild. I figured there would be more hikers since the weather was good, but we hadn't seen a soul.

It was late afternoon when we found our tent site. We cleared out all the rocks and limbs and pitched the tent. We had a neat little tent. It slept four, and it had a small divider. Dad always wanted to make sure that, me being a girl, I had my privacy. But the tent wasn't tall, so you just crawled in and slept. This way there wasn't a lot of extra weight to carry.

"I'll catch supper and you start a fire." Dad pulled his handy dandy folding fishing pole out of his pack and headed for the stream.

The fire ring we always used had some washout, so I set to getting it back in shape as Matthias picked up broken branches and limbs. I was pretty sure he had made many fires in his lifetime by the way he laid the wood. Soon, he had a nice fire going. Dad caught four nice fish and had them skinned and ready to cook in no time. He then got out his little aluminum skillet and started cooking them. It only held two at a time, but that was fine. Dad insisted we eat first while he cooked the other two. They were good. Plain, but good. I lay back on the ground and watched the sun fade behind the horizon. The night was clear and a little cool, perfect for camping. I grabbed my bag and headed toward the stream.

"I'll be back in a few, going to wash up a bit."

"Yell if you need anything," Dad said.

I smiled. "I will." I could hear Dad and Matthias talking about the stars. Dad loved to look at the stars and knew most of the constellations. I am sure Matthias probably knew more than Dad, but he wouldn't let on. I trudged up and around the bend. There was a nice little deep spot I always came to. It wasn't very big, but just right for washing the day's grime off. The water was a bit chilly, but to be clean was well worth the chill. I heard a wolf howl in the distance. I glanced up. "I agree. The moon is beautiful," I chuckled. Soon I was clean and dried off and back into clothes. I didn't pack clothes I could do without, that just added weight, so pj's were out. I could hear Matthias laugh as I came around the bend. There was no telling what Dad was saying to him. They both looked at me as I walked up, and then busted out in laughter again. Great, he was telling stories about me.

"I don't want to know, so just keep it to yourselves." That just made them both howl more. I put my bag back in the tent at started cleaning up from our fish. Being out with wild animals, you had to take extra precautions with food. I took all the bones and yuck that Dad had skinned off the fish and buried it in a small hole away from the tents. Matthias took a rope and hung the backpack, with what little food we had brought, in a tree. Dad cleaned the pan and put it away. Dad headed off to wash up. I leaned back on a rock.

"You looked like quite the expert making that fire."

He laughed. "I have made several in my lifetime." We both giggled.

"I talked to Daniel last night." That caught his attention. He came and sat down beside me.

"Did he give you a big speech, too?" he asked.

"No, I gave him something to think about before we got to talk."

He looked at me. "What did you do?"

"Well, I sort of pinned him to the ceiling."

"You did what?"

"I didn't mean to. I was dreaming and he woke me, but not before I pinned him to the ceiling."

That took him by surprise. "You assaulted him again?"

I smiled. "No, I was pissed off in my dream and he hit the ceiling, but I hadn't moved. I was still on the bed."

"So what did he say about that?" He smiled.

"What could he say? I had him pinned, so he had to listen to me."

"And?" he asked.

"Well, he said he didn't really know what was going on, but he wasn't going to try to stop it."

He slid his arm around my neck and pulled close to me. "So he wasn't angry or anything?"

"No, he didn't seem to be." I could feel the tension leave his body. I laid my head over on him and relaxed.

"Next." Dad came into view.

Matthias removed his arm and got his stuff. "So where is it that you guys are going?"

Dad and I both laughed. "Follow the stream around the bend. There is a big boulder and beside it is a little pool of water, about four feet deep," Dad told him. He smiled and headed out into the darkness. I was sure he would just probably go out of sight and do that thing he did.

"This has been great, Dad. Thanks."

He smiled and sat down. "I've missed it, too."

"So you think Matthias likes it? He seems quite comfortable out here. I guess it's the Indian blood in him."

"I think you're right. He does fit in quite well." We sat back and watched the stars sparkle. They reminded me of Matthias and Daniel and the sparkly glow they put off.

"Hey, you know if you go up a little farther there is a bigger pool?" Matthias said as he reappeared. So he had been exploring.

"I am turning in," I announced as I stood up.

"Sounds good," Dad agreed. I crawled into my side and stretched out. I couldn't help but giggle at all the "Oops, sorrys" coming from the other side of the tent. Matthias was a pretty big guy; it was a good thing Dad wasn't. I waited until I heard Dad start to snore before I closed my eyes. I was sure that as soon as the first snore left Dad's lips, Matthias was gone. I felt Daniel's warm hand on my cheek and slid off to sleep.

I woke to Daniel's soft voice. *"I have to leave before your Dad wakes up. He is getting pretty restless."*

I opened my eyes. *"I'm up."* He vanished. I could hear the trees rustling in the breeze. I wiggled out of the tent as the sun was just rising. Matthias was sitting on a rock poking at the ashes left from the fire last night. I walked over, sat in front of him, and leaned back on the rock.

"Sleep well?"

"Not bad, missed my soft bed, but all in all it wasn't bad. So what did you do all night?" He chuckled. "What did you do?"

"I went back to your house, did the laundry." I looked at him. "Oh that took all of five seconds." He smiled. "I lay on your bed, watched a couple of movies, listened to some music, just that kind of stuff."

Dad gave a big yawn. "He lives." We both laughed. Dad came crawling out. We both looked over his way.

"You guys are up early."

"No," I said. "You slept late. You missed the sunrise."

Matthias got up and got the pack down from the tree. "Anybody up for a muffin?" He pitched one each to Dad and me and took one himself. I went and got water bottles out of the tent.

After breakfast, we took down the tent and poured water on the ashes in the fire pit to make sure they were good and out. When we were all packed up, Dad led the way down the trail. We stopped a couple of times so Dad could point out some tree or landmark. Matthias took it in stride and asked questions for Dad's sake. About noon, Dad stopped.

"I don't remember this trail." There was a fork in the trail in front of him. I couldn't remember it either. "You want to try the new one?" Dad asked.

"Go for it, Dad," I said, and off we went. It went north for a good five miles then made a turn east. The trail was pretty smooth, but really narrow. At just about five miles, it led out onto a meadow. I knew where we were and so did Matthias.

"I would say we could camp here, but I don't know where we are or how far we are from the entrance. I think this trail threw me off."

Matthias smiled. "The entrance to the park is five miles due south." He turned to look at him.

"You let me go on and on and you've been here before?"

He gave Dad a big smile. "I have been to this meadow before, but not much farther. There is a small dirt road on the other side of the meadow that I always come up. It will take you back to the city, or there's a trail over there that will take you back to the park entrance."

Dad gave him the eye as if to see if he were lying. "Alright, then." He finally seemed to accept what he said. "How about we camp here then?" I wanted to say no, I couldn't imagine being in the meadow after dark. On the other hand I had been here before, with Matthias, and nothing had happened; but it wasn't night then either.

"Sure." I started picking up little twigs and stuff so we could pitch the tent. Dad sat down his pack and got the tent out. It took no time to get it up. Matthias and I went to the streambed to get some rocks to make a fire ring.

"What's wrong?" Matthias asked as we picked up rocks.

"I do not like the idea of camping here."

"It will be fine. I won't let anything happen to you" he smiled. "Nothing happened last time we were here did it?" he asked. My mind wandered back to the last time we were in the meadow.

"Well if you call it nothing" I teased him. He was right nothing had happened and it was just a dream anyway.

Once the ring was set, we gathered wood for a fire. Matthias had one lit pretty quickly. Dad rummaged through the pack to see what we could have for supper. There were some protein bars and beef jerky. I lay back on the grass and ate my bar. The sun was starting to go behind the tree line. Matthias lay down beside me.

"I am going to look for a place to wash up." Dad headed for the stream and followed it up the meadow. Matthias took my hand in his.

"I could get used to this."

I turned my head to look at him. "What, the hard ground and little food? Oh, that's right. You don't need the food or the rest." I got a little sarcastic.

He rolled up on his side to face me. "Being with you 24/7."

"Oh." I was sure my faced turned red. He let out a big laugh. "Yeah, that part is nice." I had to admit I loved him being with me all the time. He ran his finger down the side of my face. "What are you trying to do?" I rolled up on my elbow to face him. "Start a fire?"

He smiled. "Maybe." I just shook my head. I pushed him off his elbow and onto his back. I laid my head on his chest. "I could definitely get used to this," he said. I just laughed at him. A noise in the distance caught my attention.

"Do you hear that?" I asked. Was Dad coming back already? No. I sat up. It had gotten completely dark. "Dad?" No answer. Oh, crap! My heart started racing. Matthias sat up and got still to listen. I knew what it was. Was I imagining it? No, the sound got louder. Matthias seemed to be frozen to his spot. He recognized it, too. It was like a whole bunch of people screaming in horror all at once. It was my dream. I could see a small red glow on the other side of the meadow. It was slowly growing. I stood up and planted my feet.

"Go find Dad and see if he is okay." I told Matthias.

"I am not leaving you."

"It won't take you two seconds. Just give him a look."

He vanished, and the demon flashed. It was now standing right in front of me. Another flash, this one silver, came between us. Daniel stood between me and the demon. It grabbed him around the neck. A second flash of silver came from behind me and attacked the creature. A scream came out of my throat. "No!" He grabbed for Matthias. No! This was not going to happen. Their glow started to flicker. I got instantly furious. I could feel everything around me I reached out with every bit of anger I had and slung Matthias and Daniel out of the way, out of the demon's reach. I held them at the other end of the meadow. They both struggled against me, but I held tight. No disappearing. I shut them down. I locked them in place. The demon reached for me. I felt his hand on my throat. Fire burned the spot he touched. He leaned over for the kill.

Suddenly I began to shudder. I felt very strange. The demon dropped me and stepped back, but I did not fall. Suddenly, I felt as if every part of me had exploded. I saw a dark cloud rise out from around me and cover the demon. I saw him struggling to break free from the cloud as everything went black. What was going on? Had I been killed? A small glimmer of light caught my attention. It was a small glimmer of silver. I heard a new noise. I knew the sound as well as I knew the sound of the creature; it was the sound of the angel. The light got so bright I was blinded even through my closed eyes. The angel spoke in his thundering voice, "Choose." Was I dead? Had the demon killed me like he had Matthias? Was he here to give me the same chance he had given Matthias? *I choose to serve. I choose to serve.* I kept yelling in my head.

"Lindsey." I knew that voice. *"Be still and quiet."* I stopped fighting. Thunder rolled again.

"Go ... live."

The light faded and my eyes suddenly worked. I opened them. Daniel was kneeling over me. He was smiling. Something was different. His aura was bright, but it was not silver. It was blue. Matthias came into focus beside him, and his aura was blue, too. No, his was purple.

Epilogue

"What are you doing?" Matthias came up and sat down behind me on the rock. "Are you thinking about that night?"

I was. This was the place it all had happened; the very meadow in which the creator of the universe had used my so-called cancer to kill a demon. The place Matthias and Daniel had become true humans again, and the place Dad fell and hit his head so hard he missed it all. I still didn't understand it all. Why Mom had to die and why God chose me to destroy a demon, but Matthias told me just to trust God, that He knows what He's doing. "Yes." I smiled up at him.

A lot of things had changed since that night. Dad and Daniel were now in the restoration business together. Matthias had taken Dad's advice about becoming a chef and had gone to culinary school. And, Matthias and I had gotten married, just a month after that night. Now I looked at our four-year-old twins, Kyle and Kara, running around the meadow playing with their granddad and uncle. I was a full-time mom. Matthias slid his arms around my waist. It had been over six years since that night. We may have lost all our powers, but we had gained a life together. Matthias leaned over and put his lips on mine. He still set a fire in me every time he kissed me, and even though we never lifted off the ground, our hearts still lifted into the sky.

Ten years later ... A New Beginning

"I had another dream last night, Mom. So what does a red aura mean?"

Mom looked up from her book. "Are you sure it was red?" she asked as she closed her book.

"Yeah, I'm sure! Is it a sign of evil or something?" Mom had managed to get up and wobble her way across the living room to the bar where I sat eating breakfast. Being eight months pregnant, she was now wobbling instead of walking.

"Do you think it's about time we told them, Matthias?" Mom was now talking to Dad, who had made his way out of the kitchen to help mom sit down on the edge of a barstool to my left. Kyle, my twin brother, was sitting on my right. Kyle looked at me.

"What do you think they have to tell us?" he casually asked, in my head so Mom and Dad couldn't hear him.

"Can you hear him?" I turned to look at Dad. Did he just ask me if I could hear Kyle? Did he hear Kyle?

LaVergne, TN USA
03 November 2010
203483LV00003B/69/P